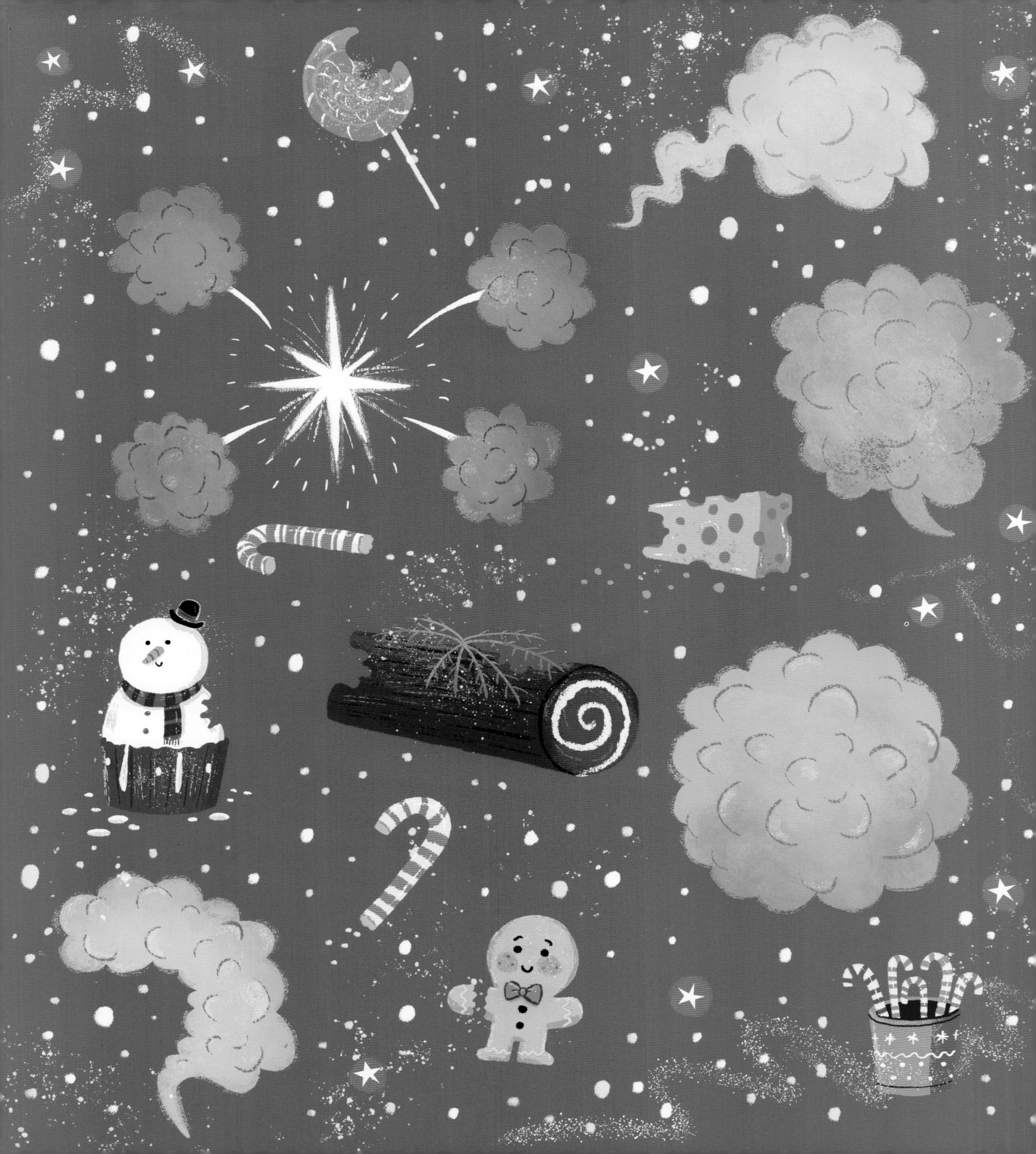

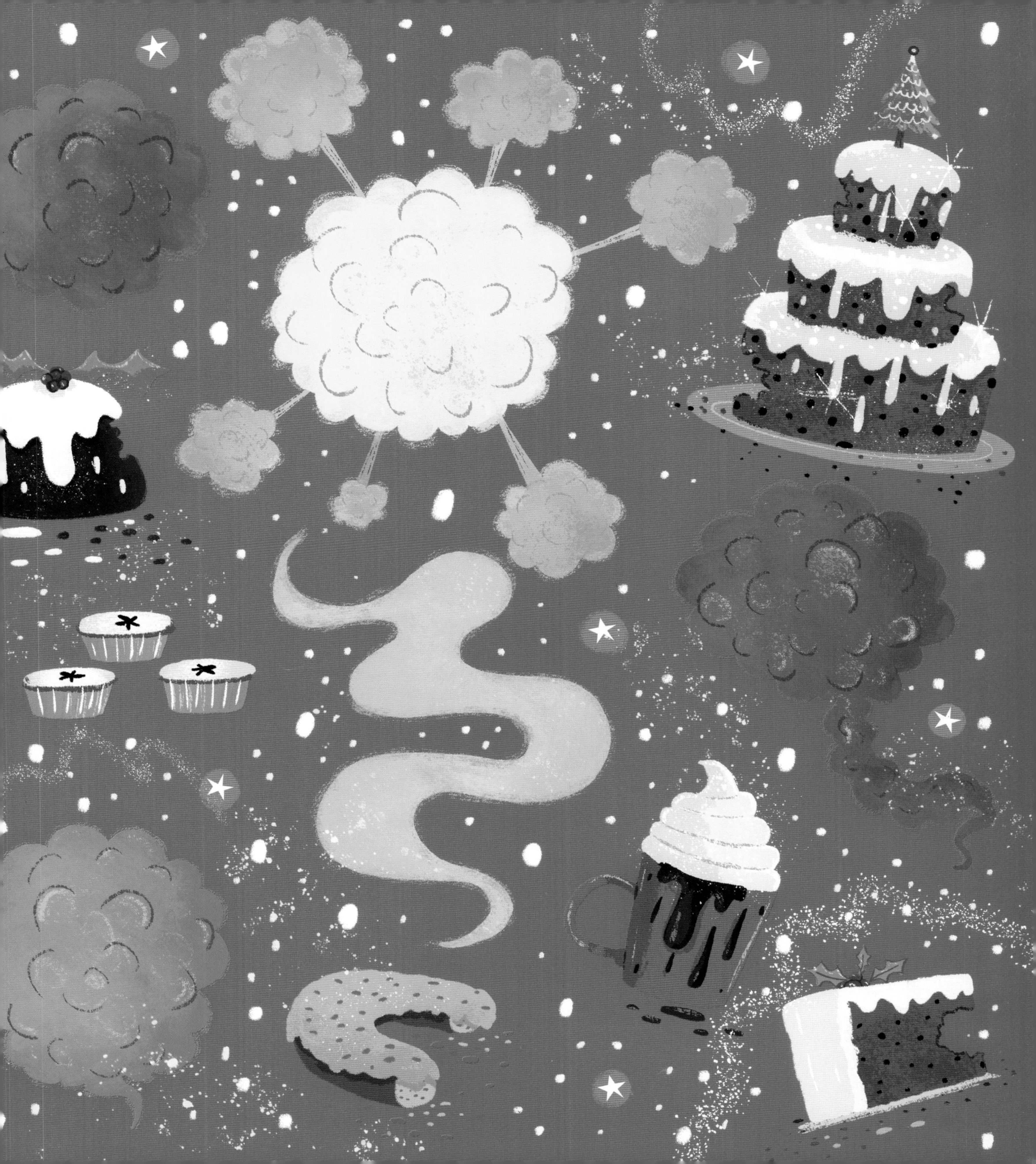

For Otto and Louis xx L.R.

For Joey, C.J.

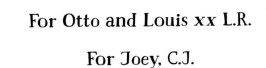

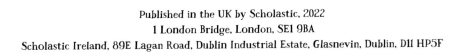

Published in the UK by Scholastic, 2022
1 London Bridge, London, SE1 9BA
Scholastic Ireland, 89E Lagan Road, Dublin Industrial Estate, Glasnevin, Dublin, D11 HP5F

SCHOLASTIC and associated logos are trademarks and/or
registered trademarks of Scholastic Inc.

ISBN 978 07023 1190 1

A CIP catalogue record for this book is available from the British Library.

Printed in China
Paper made from wood grown in sustainable forests and other controlled sources.

1 3 5 7 9 10 8 6 4 2

www.scholastic.co.uk

We Wish you a Smelly Christmas

Lucy Rowland
and Chris Jevons

SCHOLASTIC

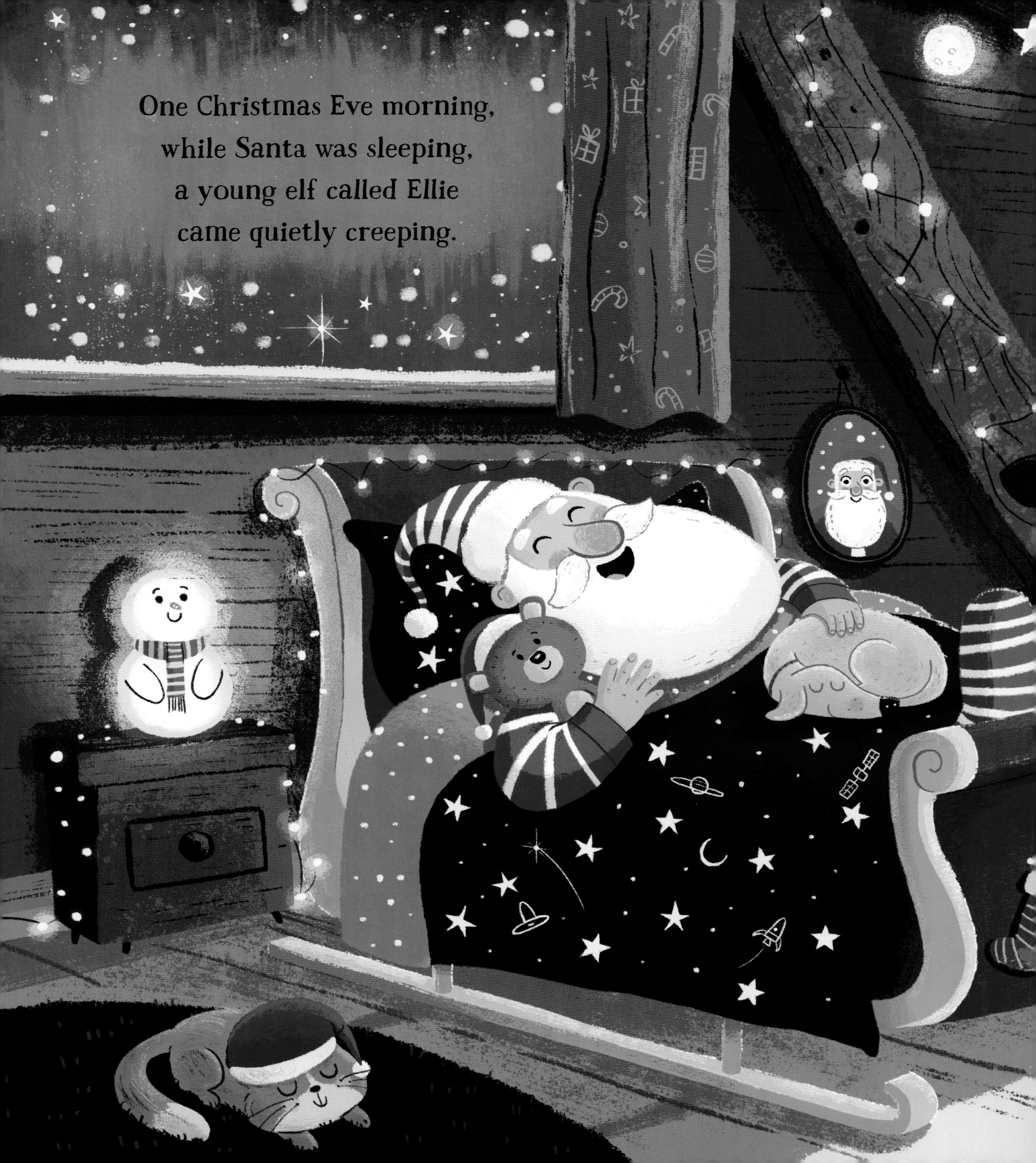

One Christmas Eve morning,
while Santa was sleeping,
a young elf called Ellie
came quietly creeping.

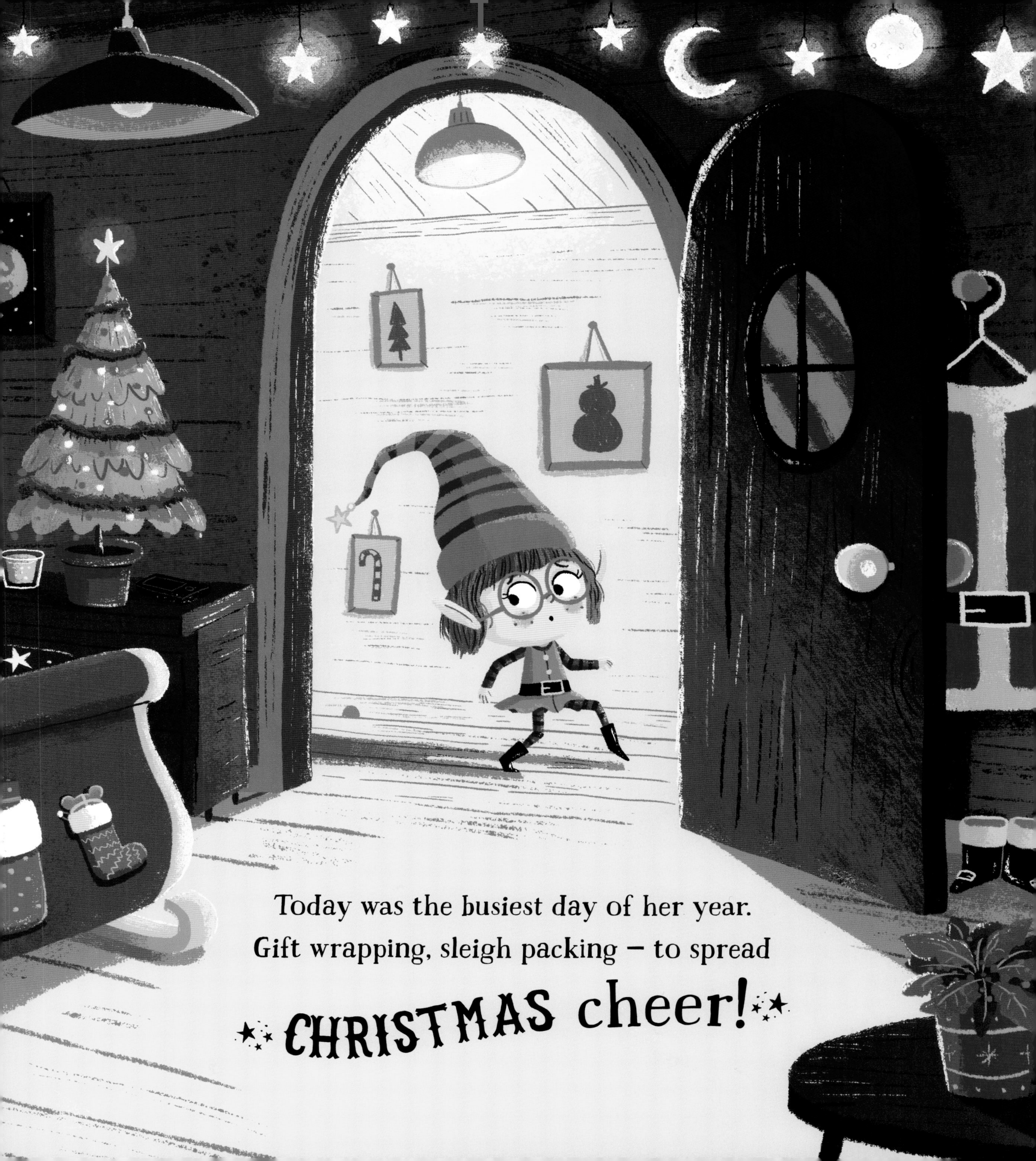

Today was the busiest day of her year.
Gift wrapping, sleigh packing – to spread
CHRISTMAS cheer!

"But what I need first," Ellie said to herself,

"is a jolly good breakfast."

She searched through the shelf.

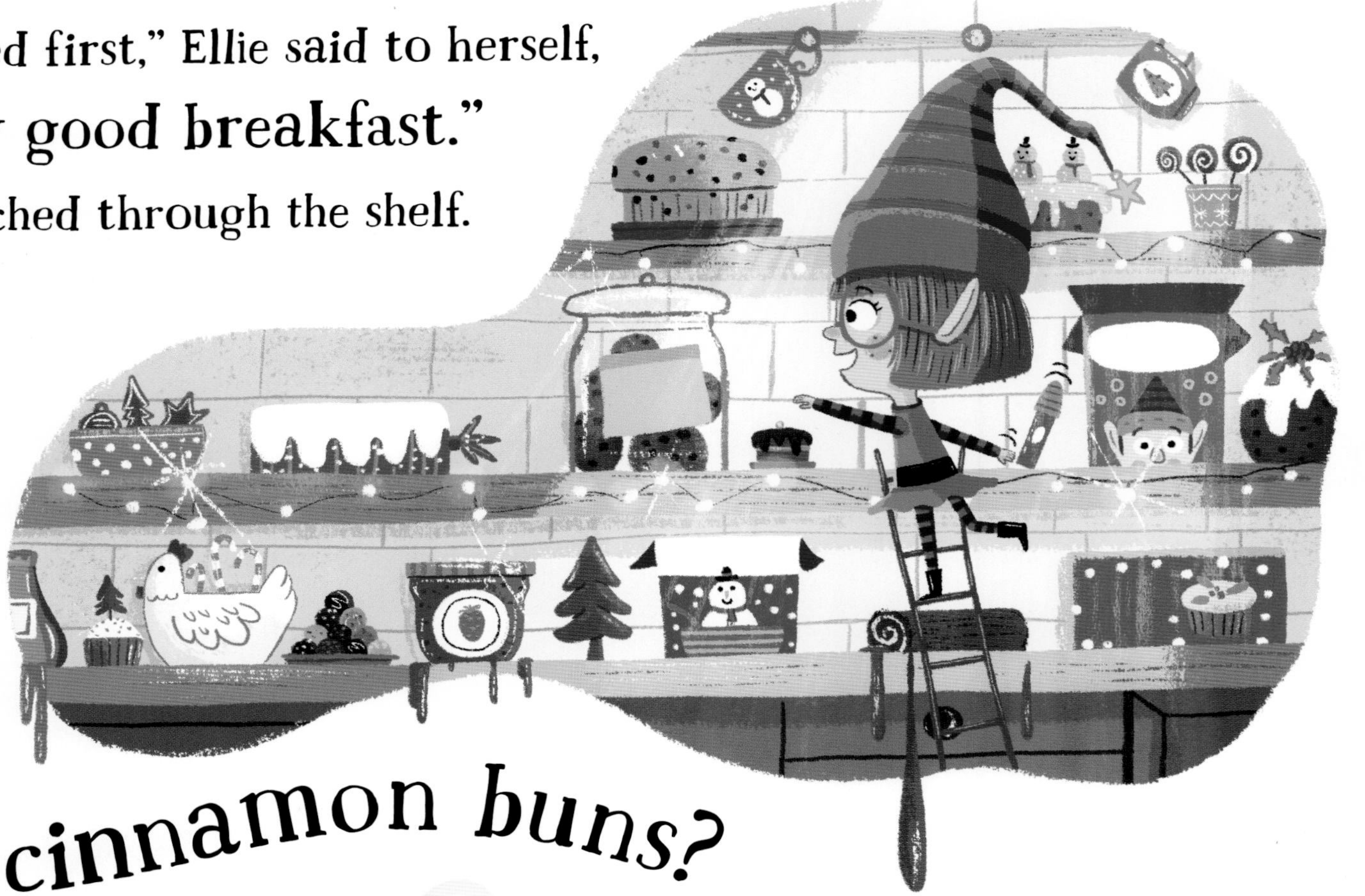

"Hot cinnamon buns?

Well, don't mind if I do!"

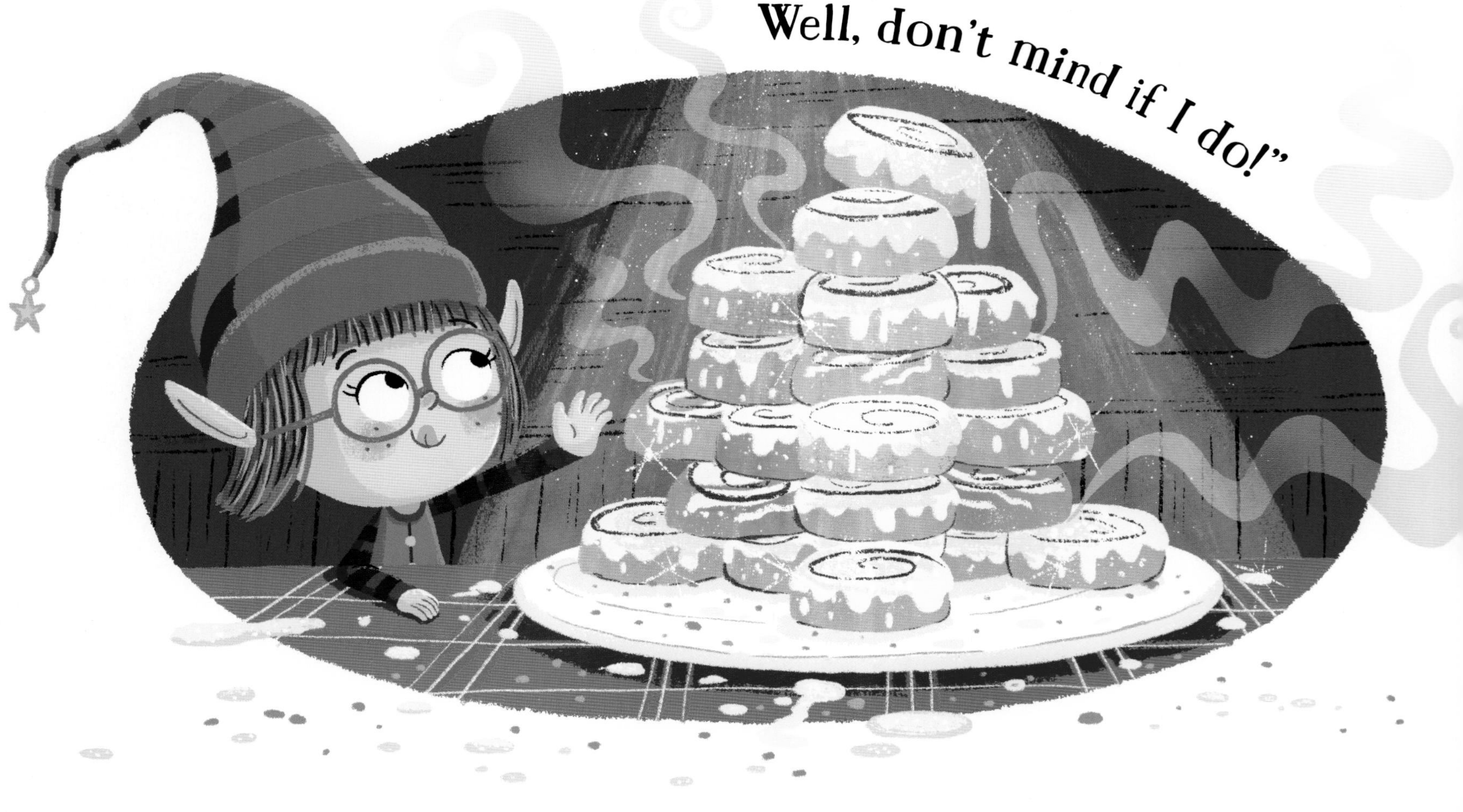

She munched
CHRISTMAS
cake

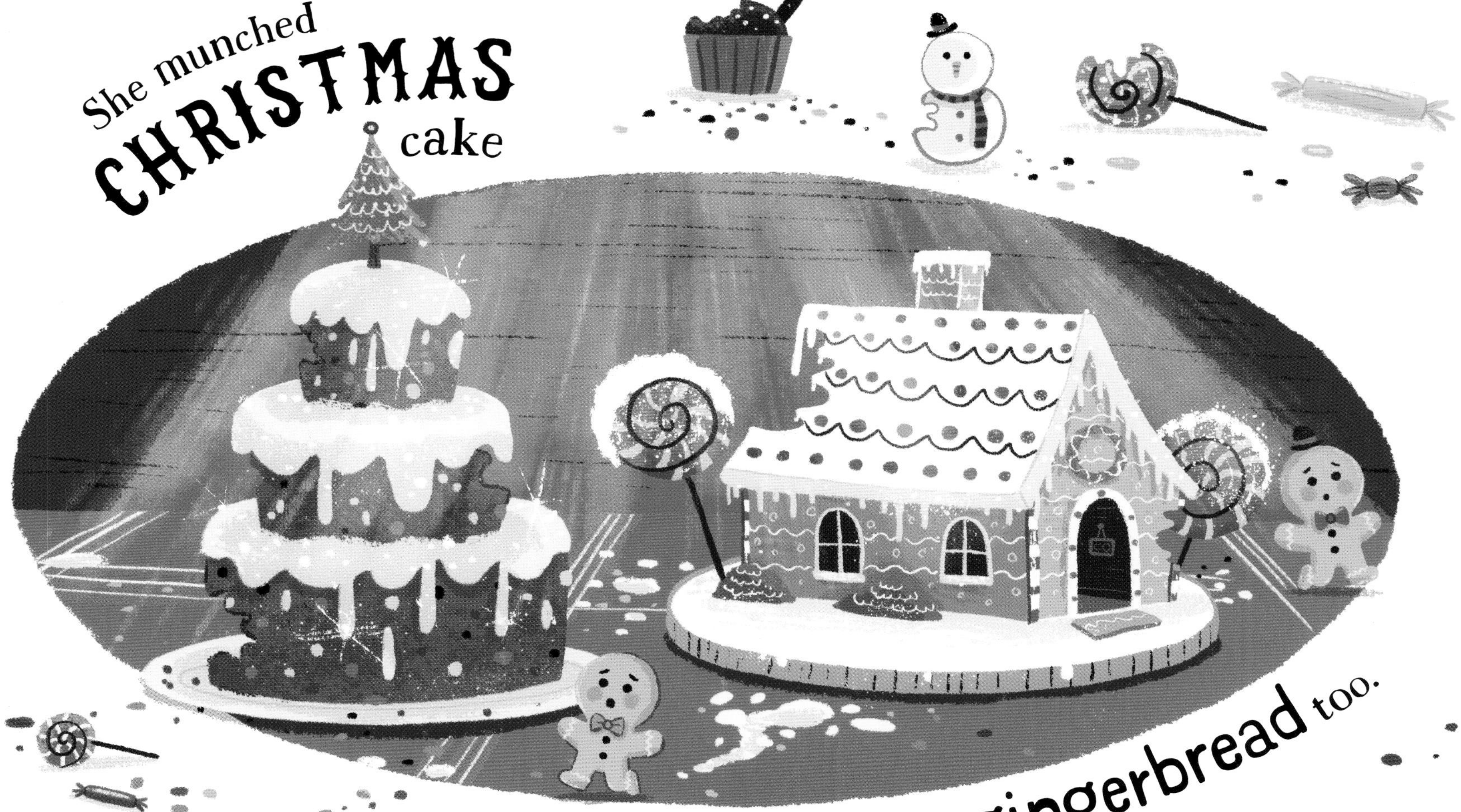

and some gingerbread too.

Next,
CANDY CANES,
mince pies,
a bottle of POP...

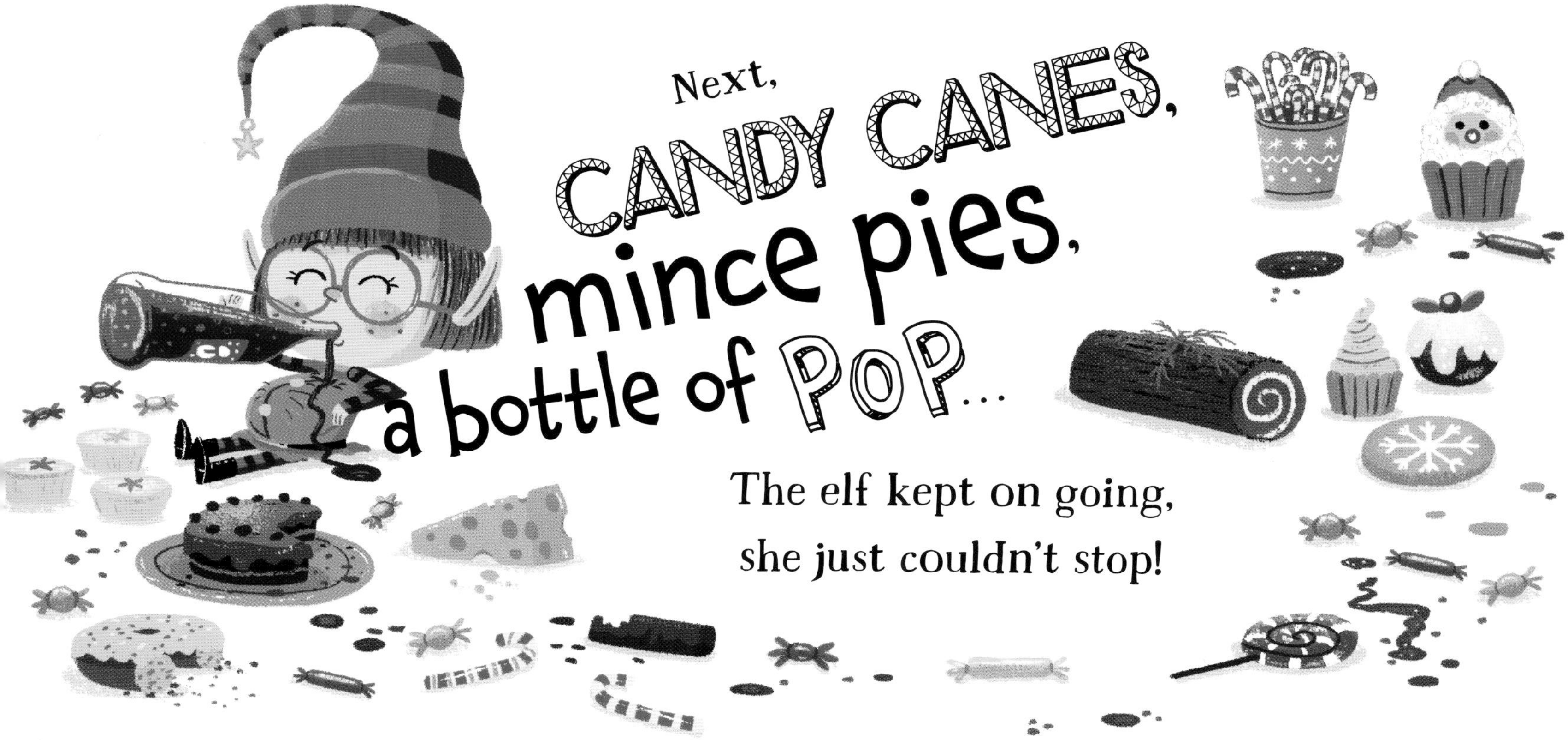

The elf kept on going,
she just couldn't stop!

At last, she crept off for a snooze in the sleigh.
The other elves gathered to start the big day.
But not too long later, there
came a strange

whiff...

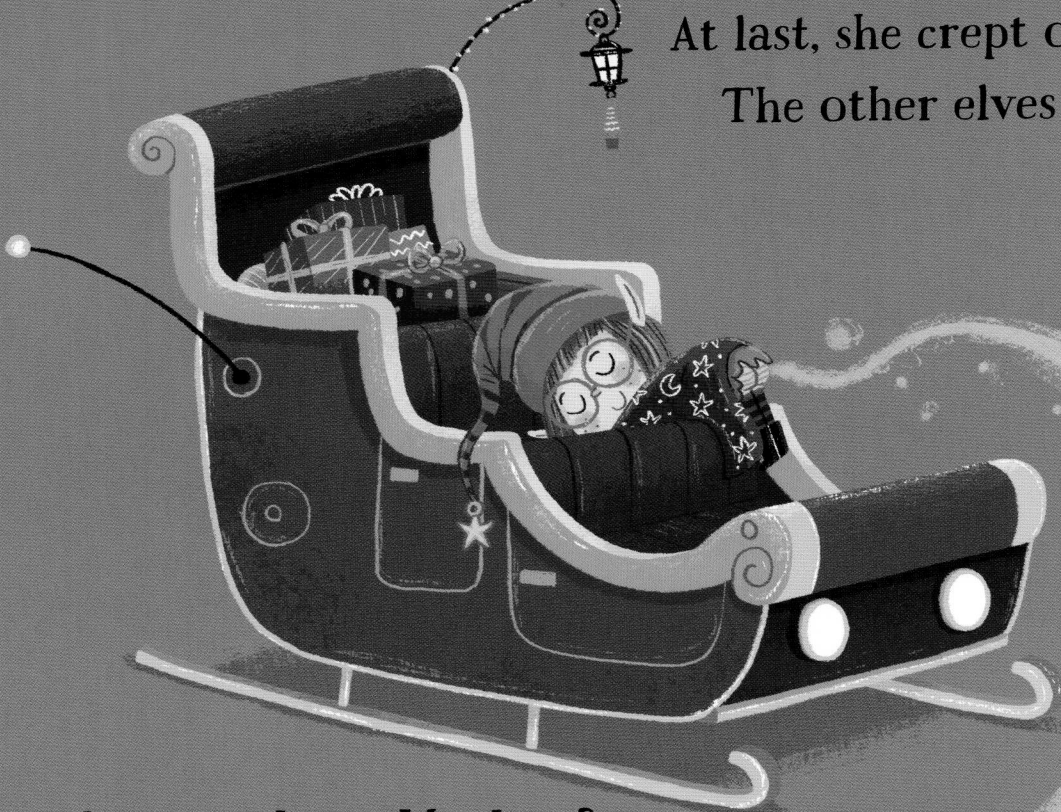

What was that odd odour?
The elves took a sniff.

"POO-EE!"

they all grumbled, while wrapping their toys.
A red-faced young elf soon awoke
to the noise.

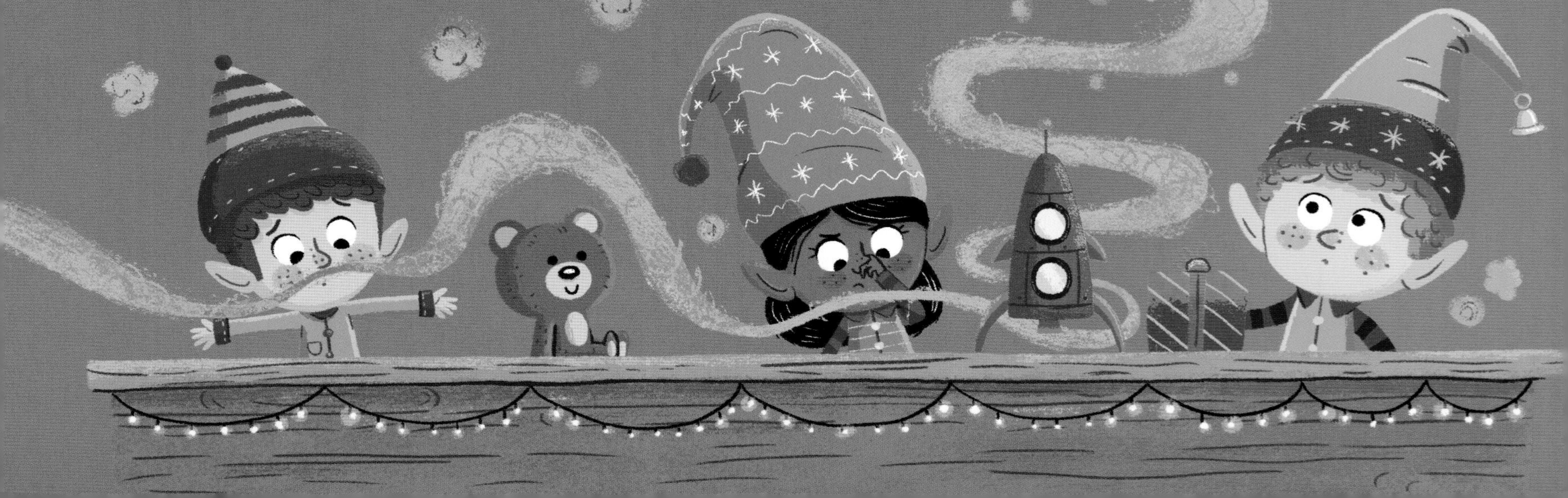

"Oh no!" Ellie gasped, "What a terrible **PONG!**"
Her belly was aching, yes, something was wrong.

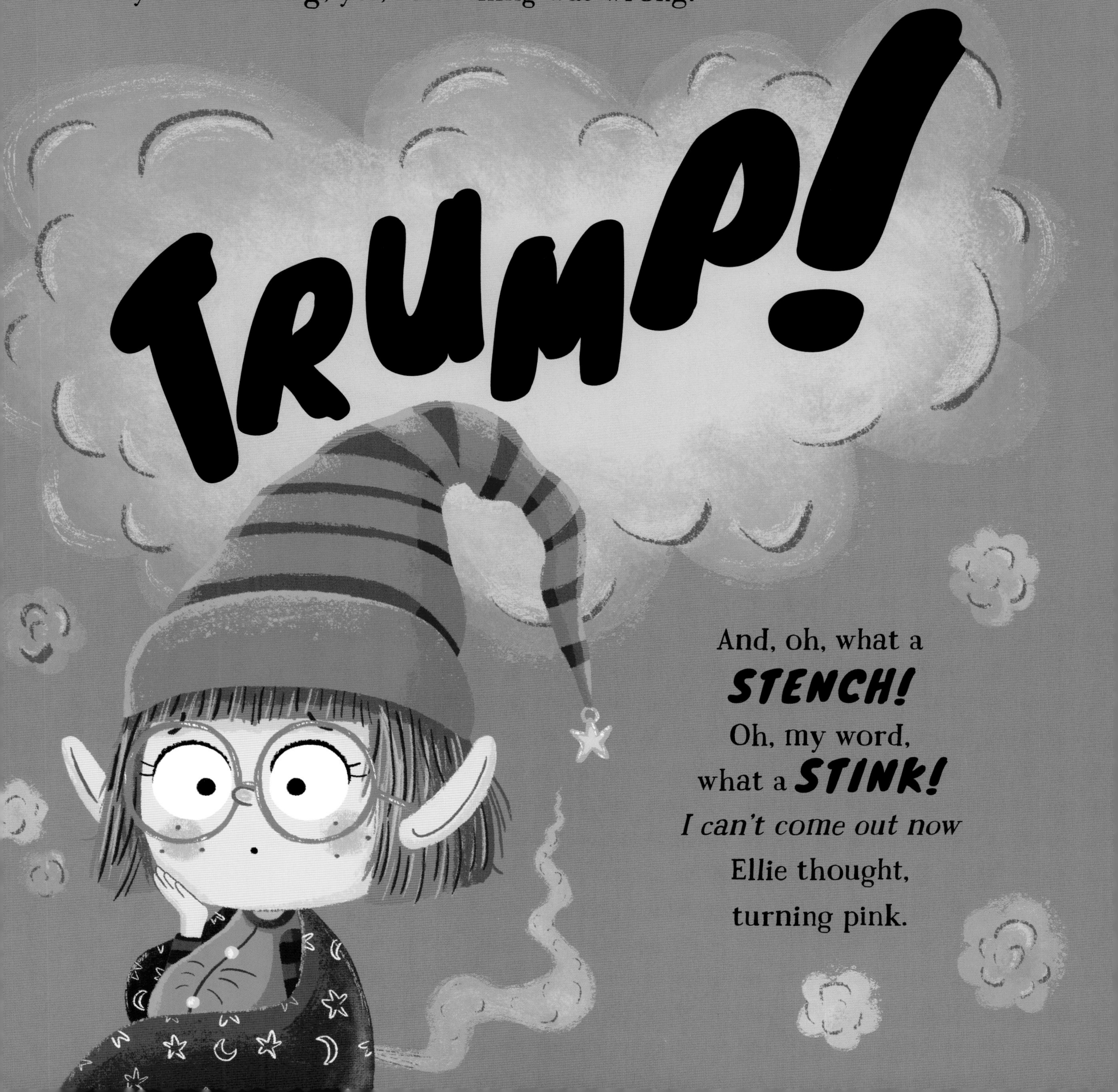
TRUMP!

And, oh, what a
STENCH!
Oh, my word,
what a **STINK!**
I can't come out now
Ellie thought,
turning pink.

TOOT!
TOOT!

TOOT!

TOOT!

TOOT!

TOOT!
TOOT!

Yes, all through the morning,
her bottom went,

TOOT!

The reindeer all chuckled.
They thought it a hoot!

Another loud **PARP** and then Santa cried "Poo!"
Poor Ellie! She just didn't know what to do.

The elves shouted

"STINKY!"

and Santa said
"VERY!
This Christmas is rather more
SMELLY than MERRY!"

But soon it was time for the reindeer to fly.
So, Santa climbed into his sleigh with a sigh.
With pegs on their noses, the reindeer took flight,
and with a loud …

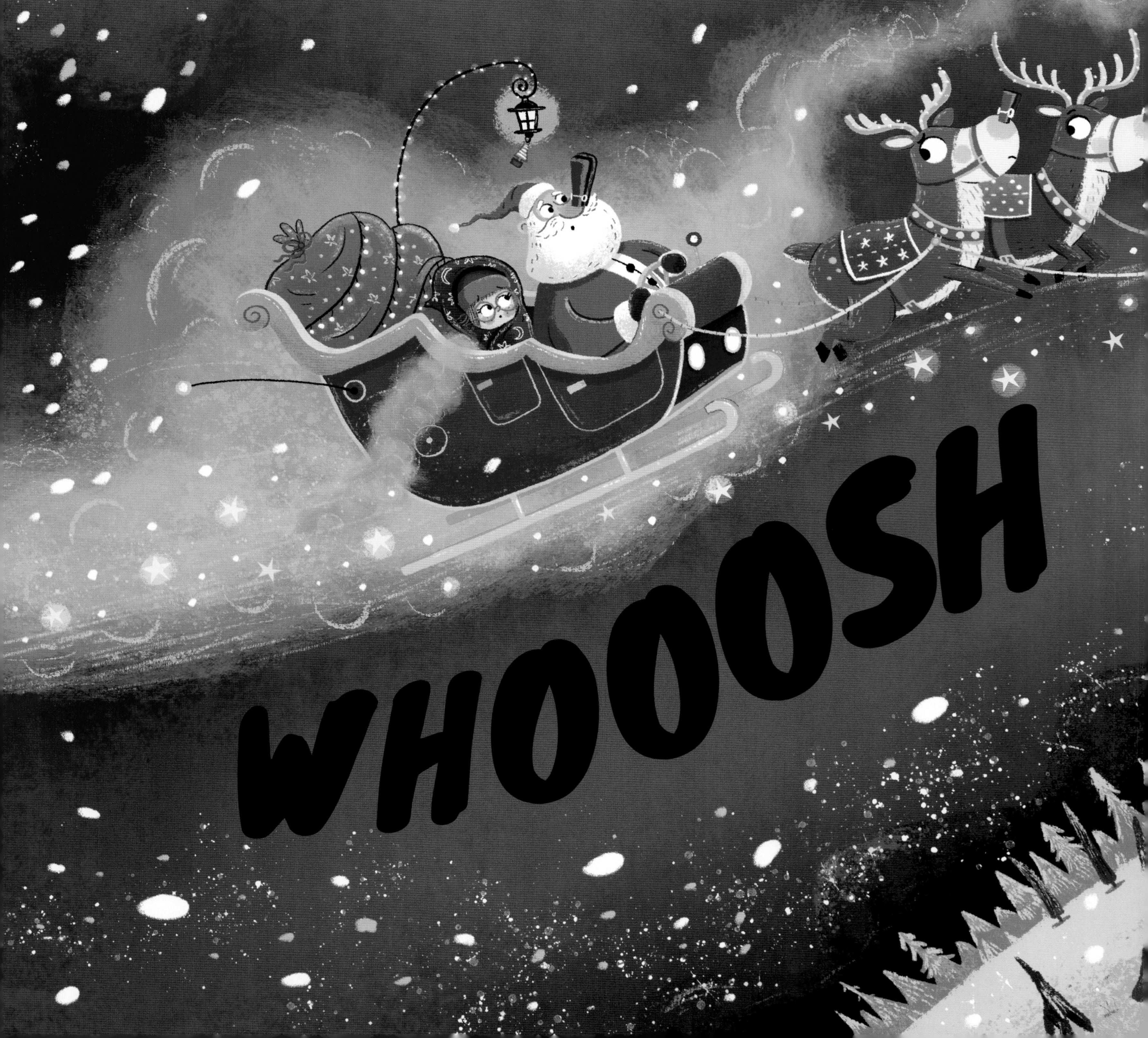
WHOOOSH

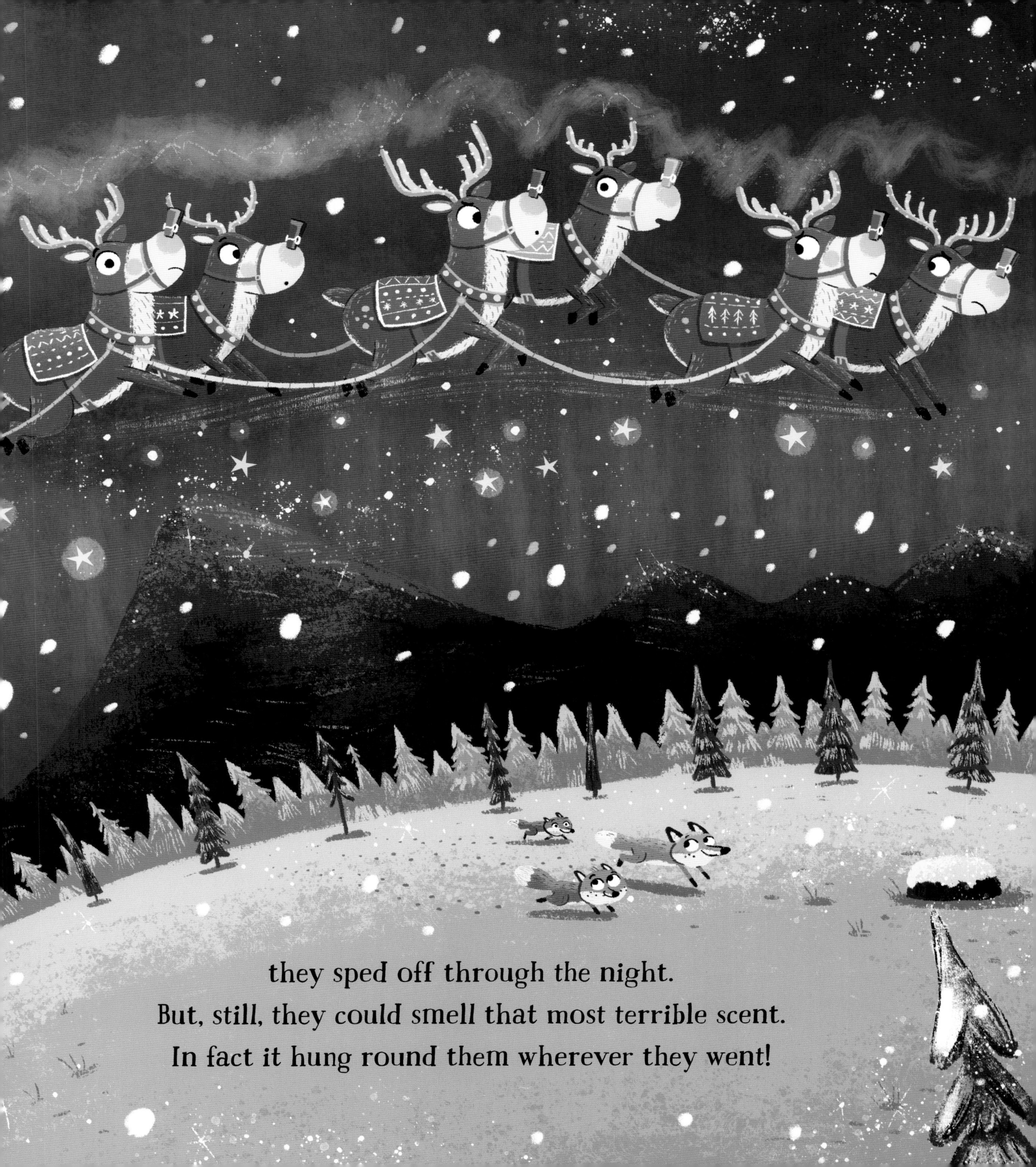

they sped off through the night.
But, still, they could smell that most terrible scent.
In fact it hung round them wherever they went!

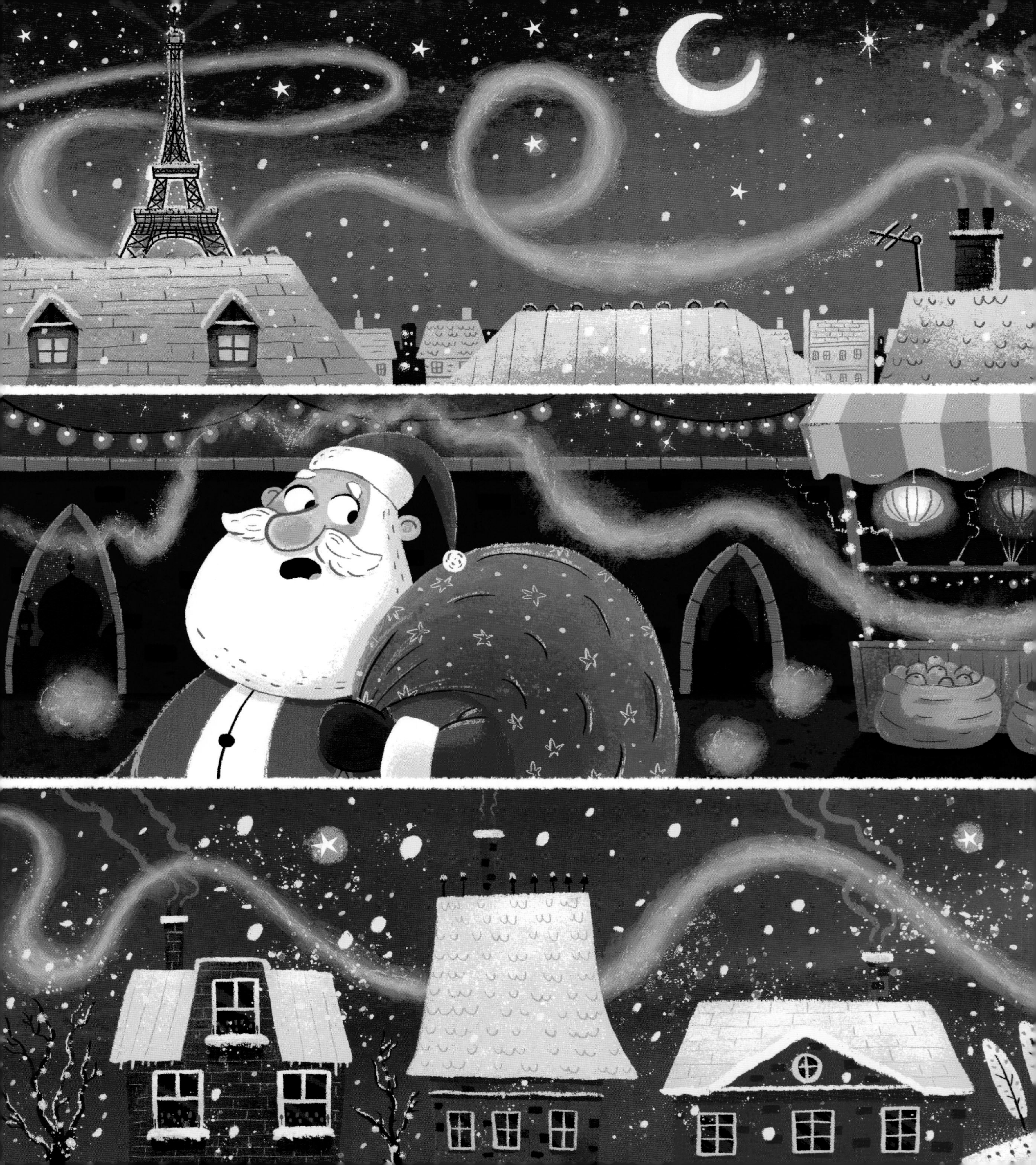

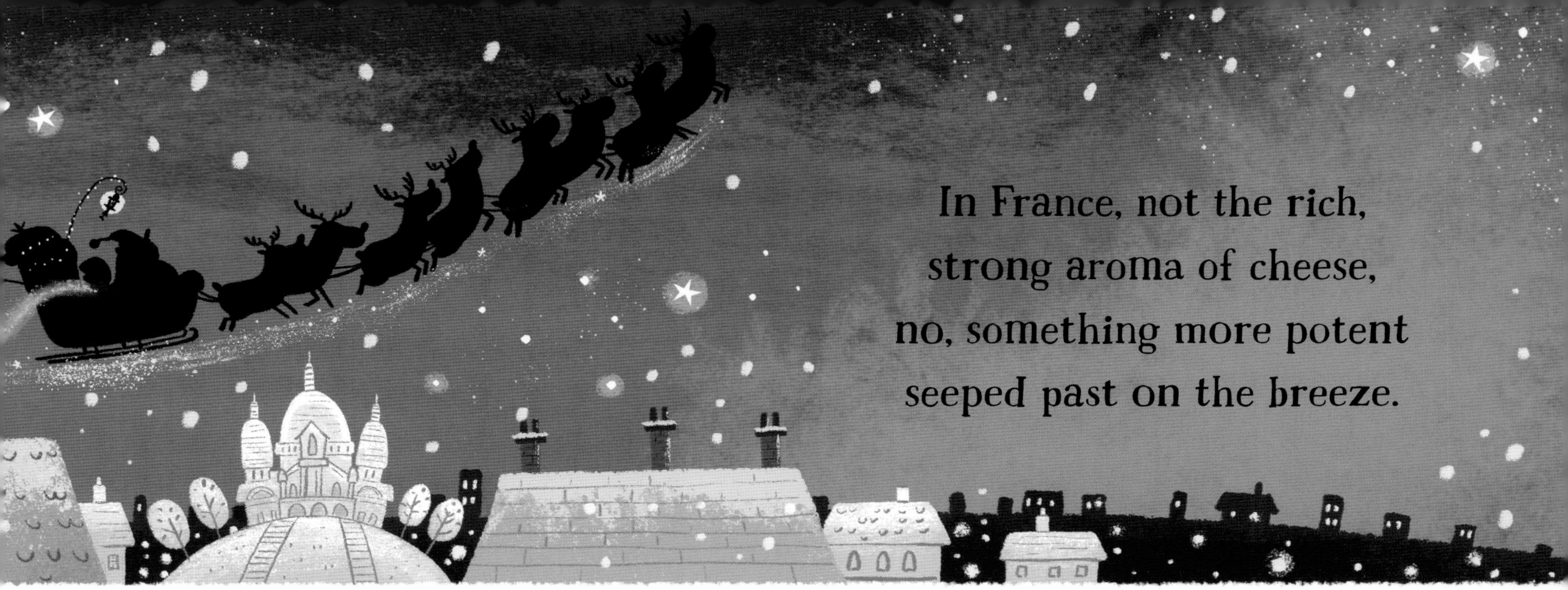

In France, not the rich,
strong aroma of cheese,
no, something more potent
seeped past on the breeze.

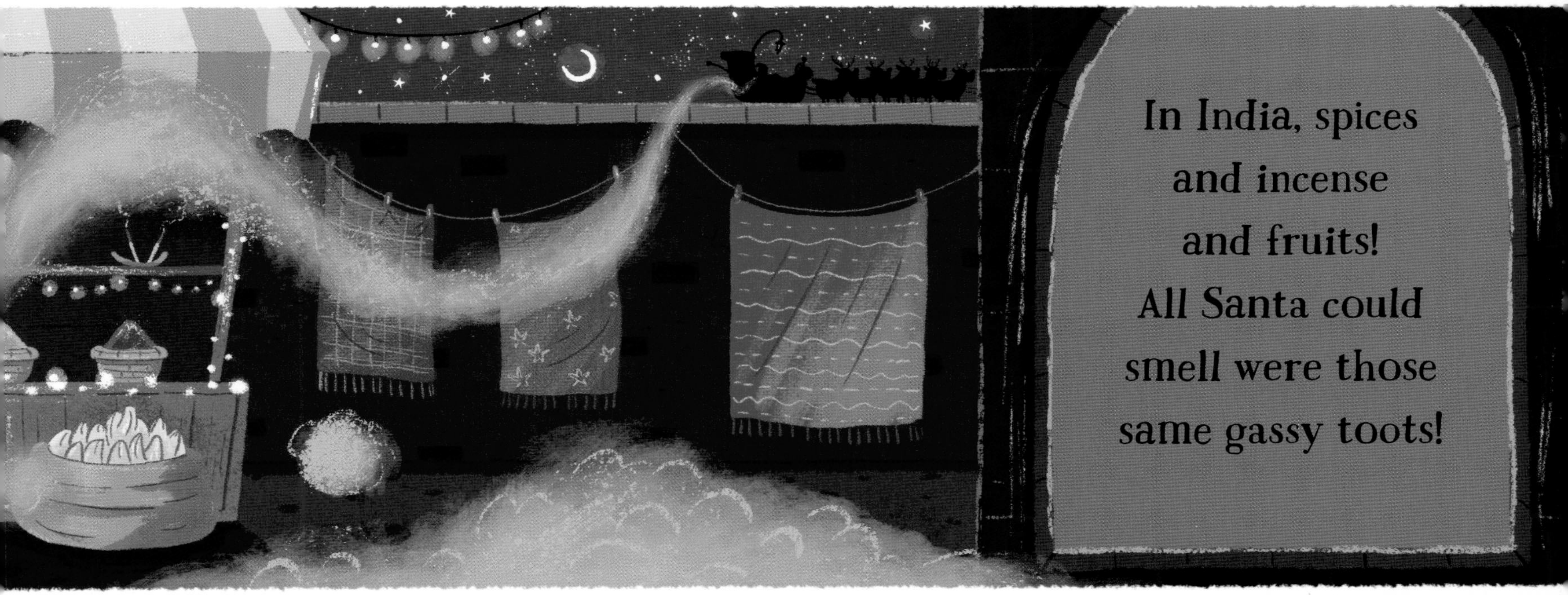

In India, spices
and incense
and fruits!
All Santa could
smell were those
same gassy toots!

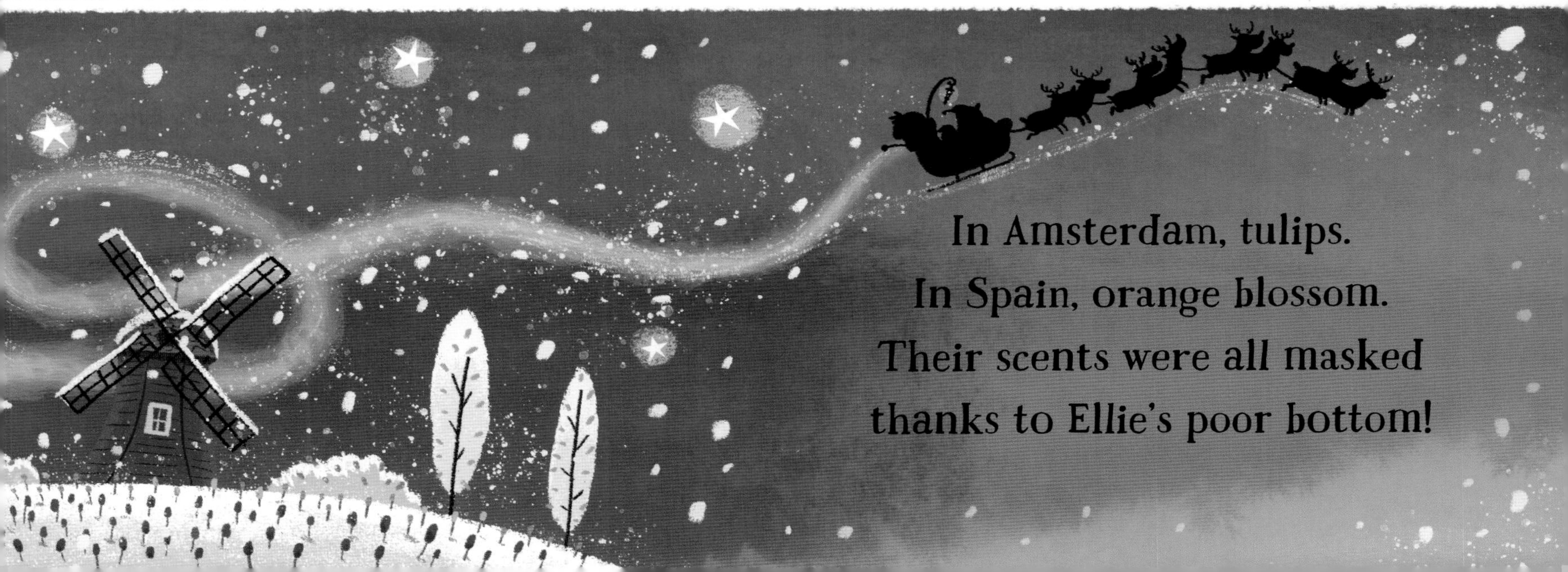

In Amsterdam, tulips.
In Spain, orange blossom.
Their scents were all masked
thanks to Ellie's poor bottom!

Now Santa was BUSY.
In village and town,
he scouted out chimneys
and scurried right down.
With so much to do,
he'd forgotten to eat,
and suddenly Santa
was craving a treat.

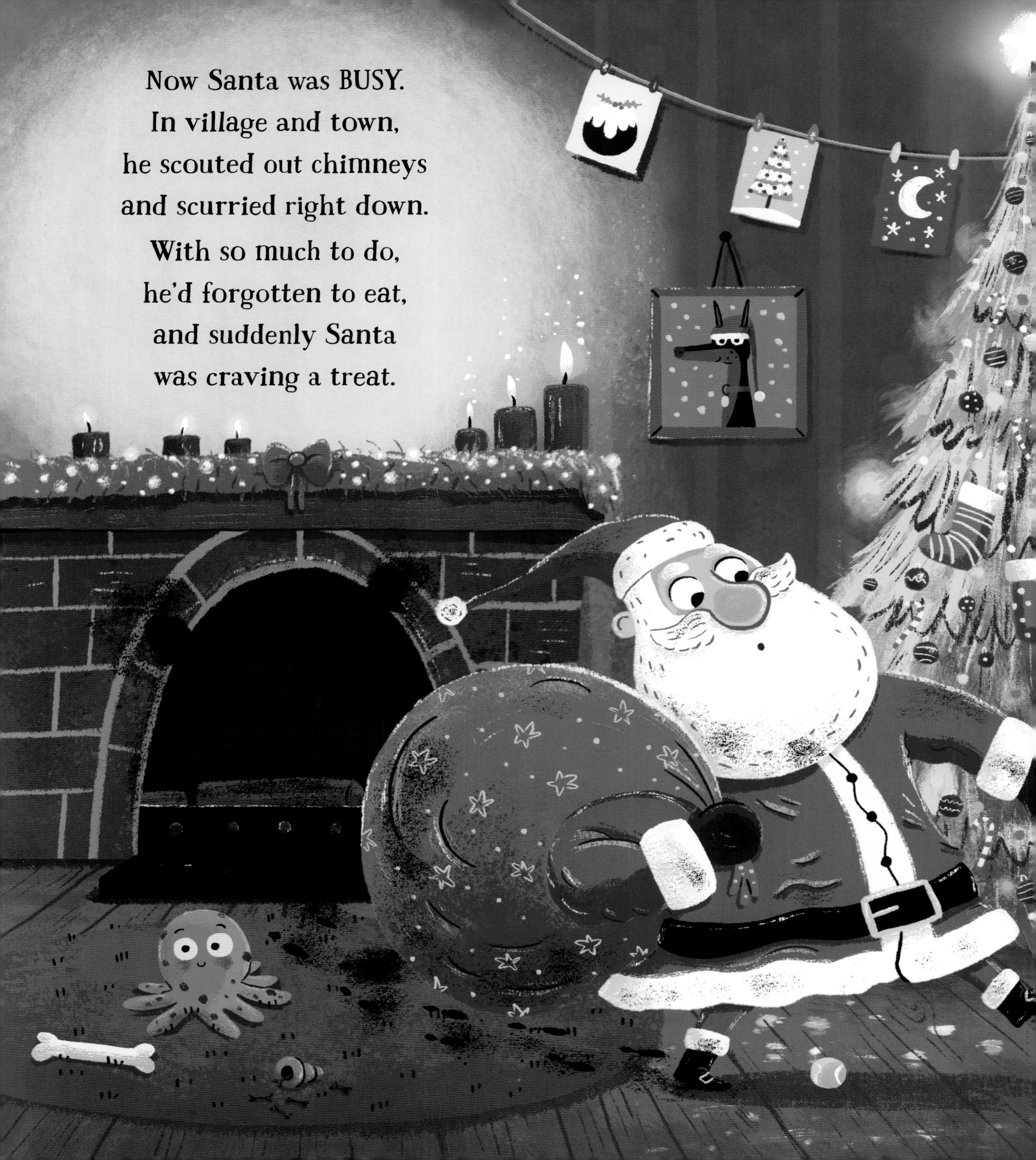

So, this year, he ate MORE mince pies than before!

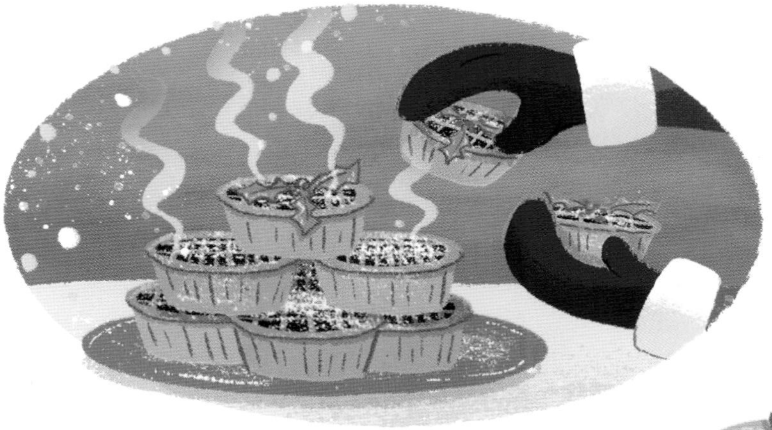

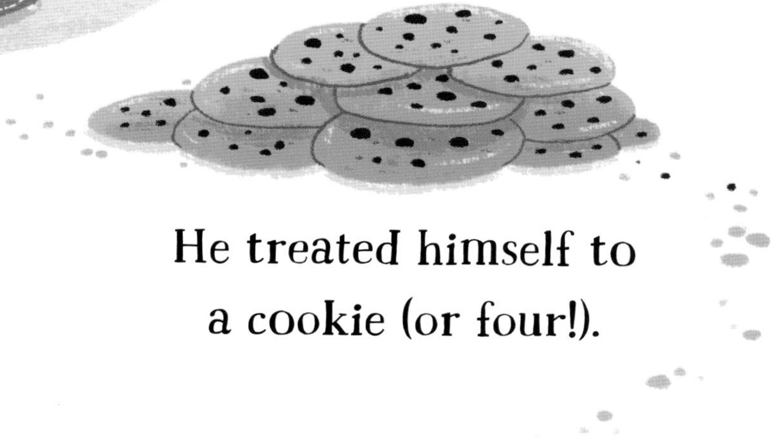

He treated himself to a cookie (or four!).

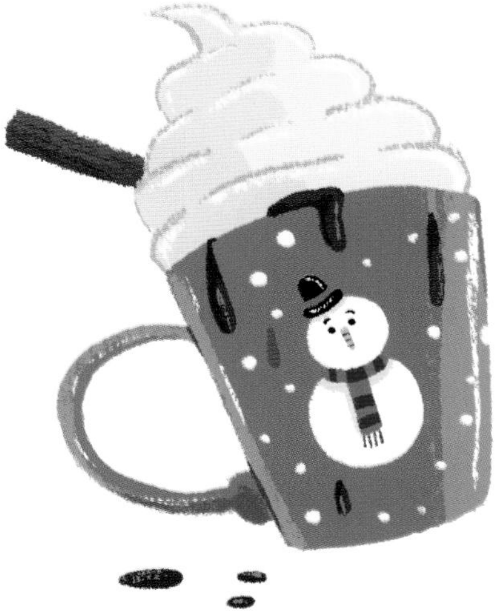

Hot chocolate and coffee, to keep him awake,

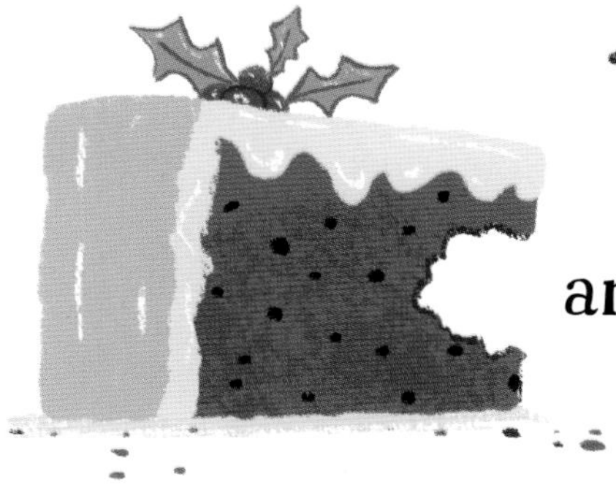

and plenty of slices of Christmassy cake.

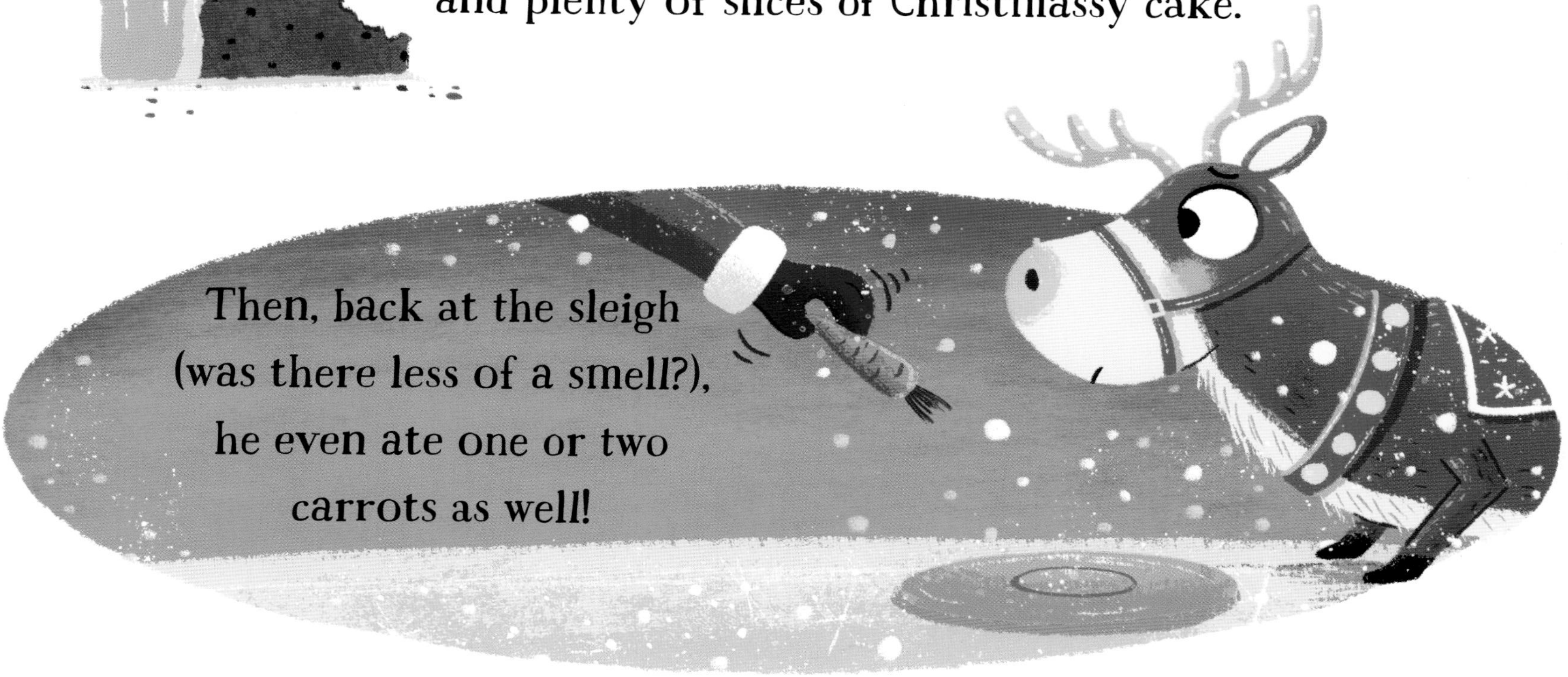

Then, back at the sleigh (was there less of a smell?), he even ate one or two carrots as well!

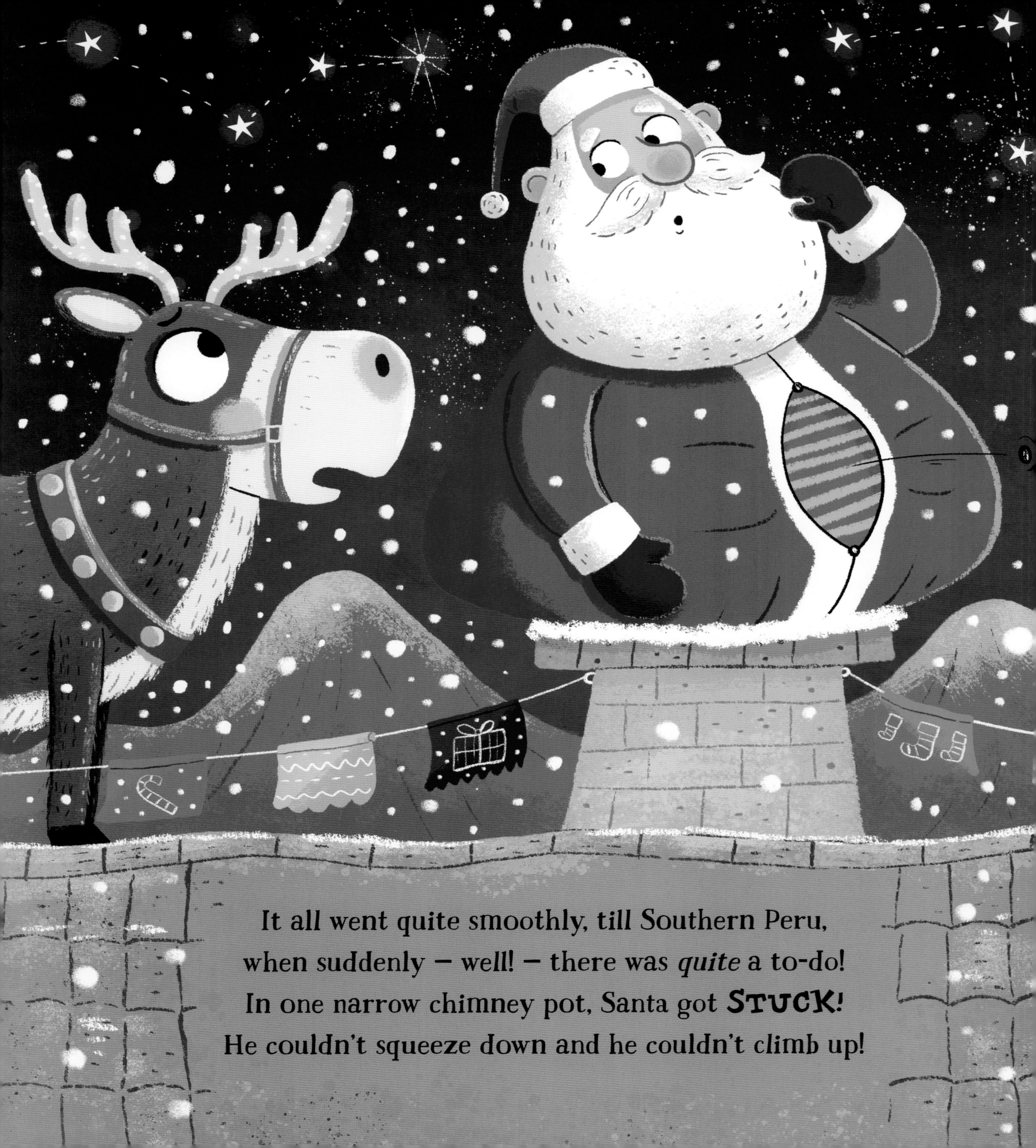

It all went quite smoothly, till Southern Peru,
when suddenly – well! – there was *quite* a to-do!
In one narrow chimney pot, Santa got **STUCK!**
He couldn't squeeze down and he couldn't climb up!

By now, Ellie Elf looked
an awful lot brighter.
Her belly was better,
she felt a bit lighter.
She'd planned to stay hidden,
but then she heard,

HELP!

Poor Santa's
in trouble!

she said with a yelp.

She rushed towards Santa but made
one last **PONG!**

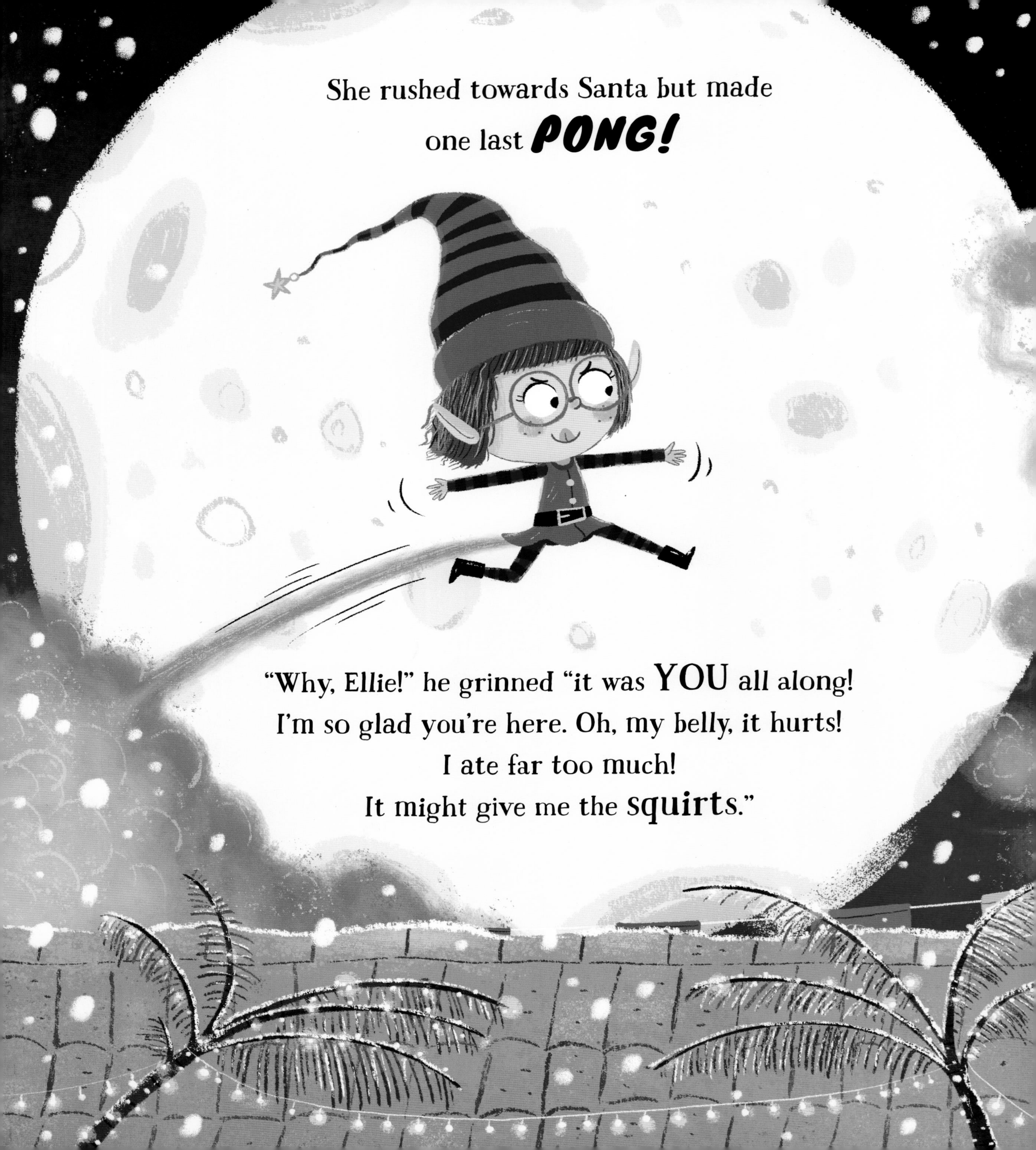

"Why, Ellie!" he grinned "it was **YOU** all along!
I'm so glad you're here. Oh, my belly, it hurts!
I ate far too much!
It might give me the **squirts**."

He let out a **TRUMP** and then chuckled

"Oh POO!"

And suddenly, Ellie knew
just what to do!

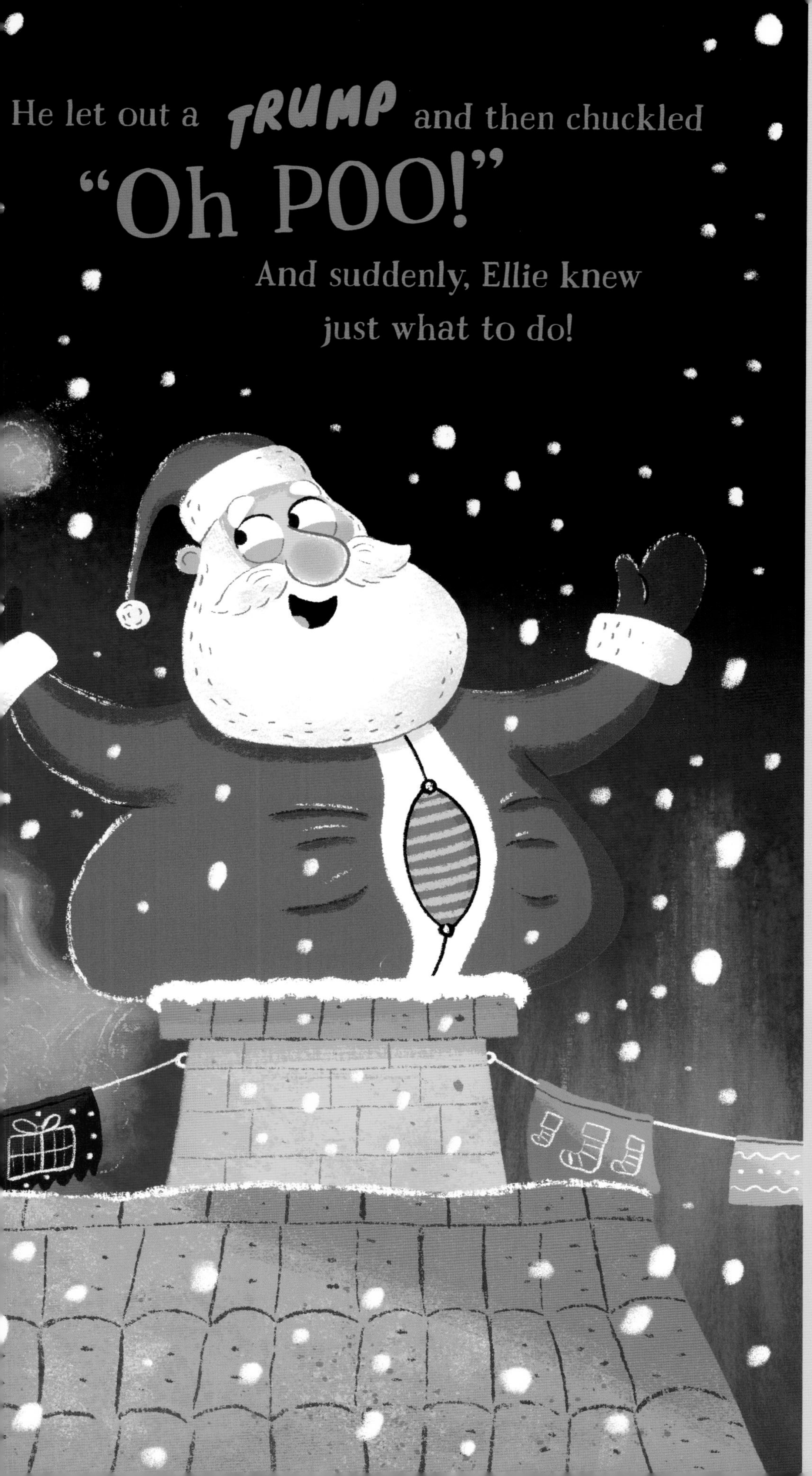

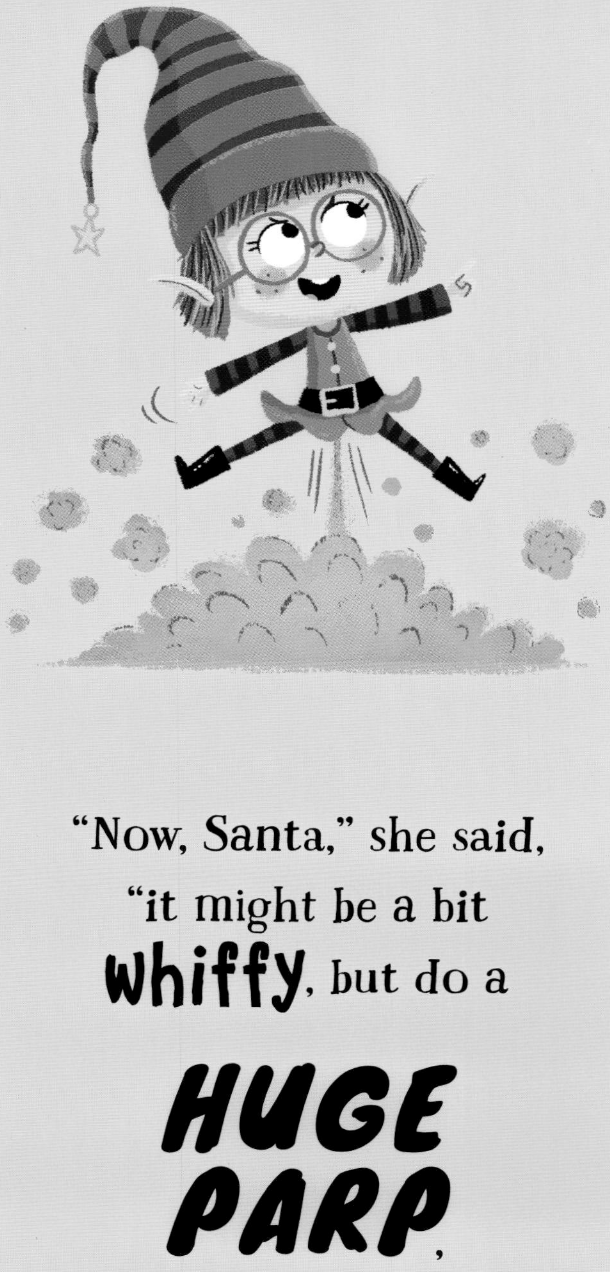

"Now, Santa," she said,
"it might be a bit
Whiffy, but do a

HUGE PARP,

you'll be out in a jiffy!
Your belly won't ache
and you'll be
on your way,

now, 1, 2, 3…

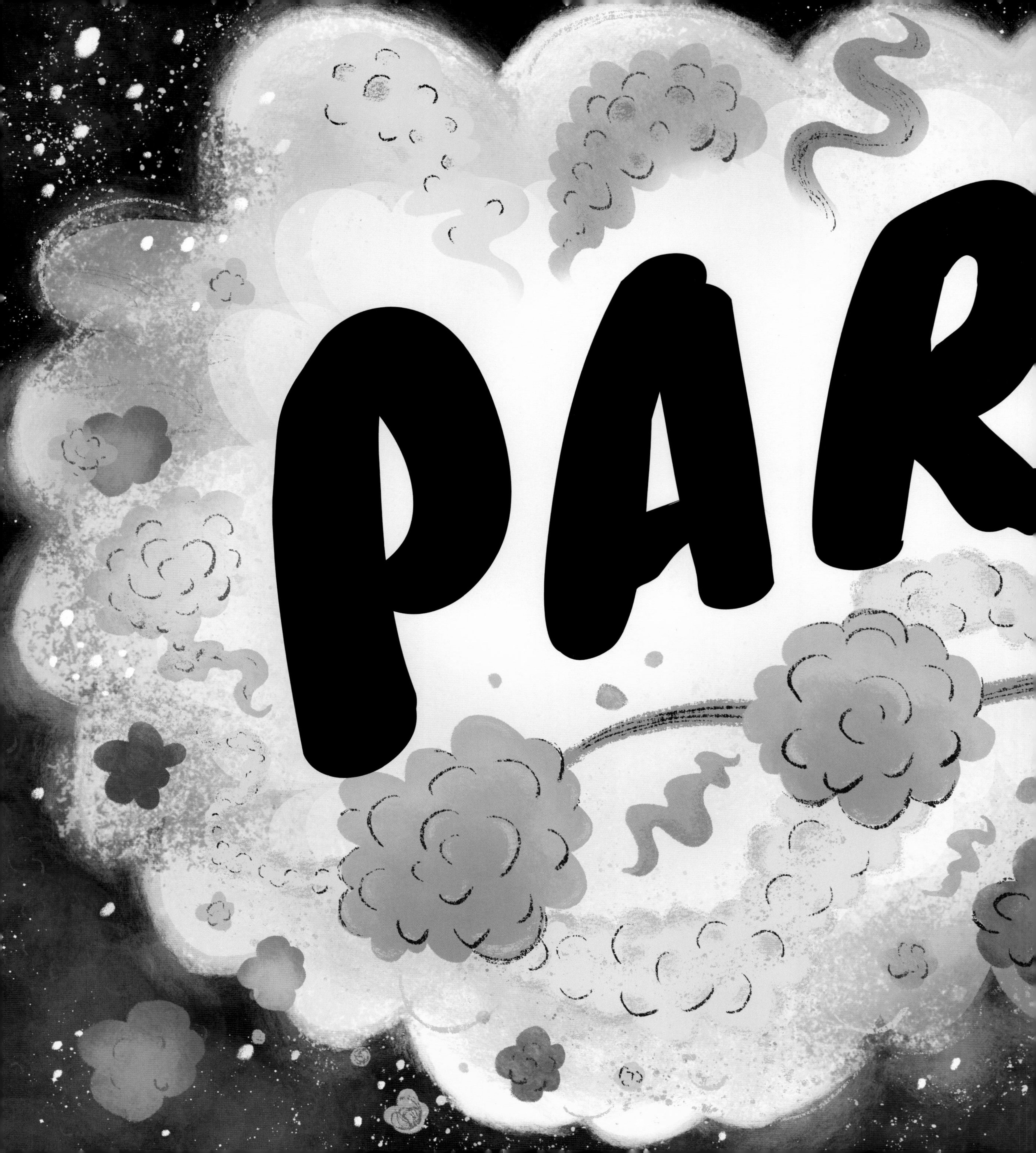
PAR

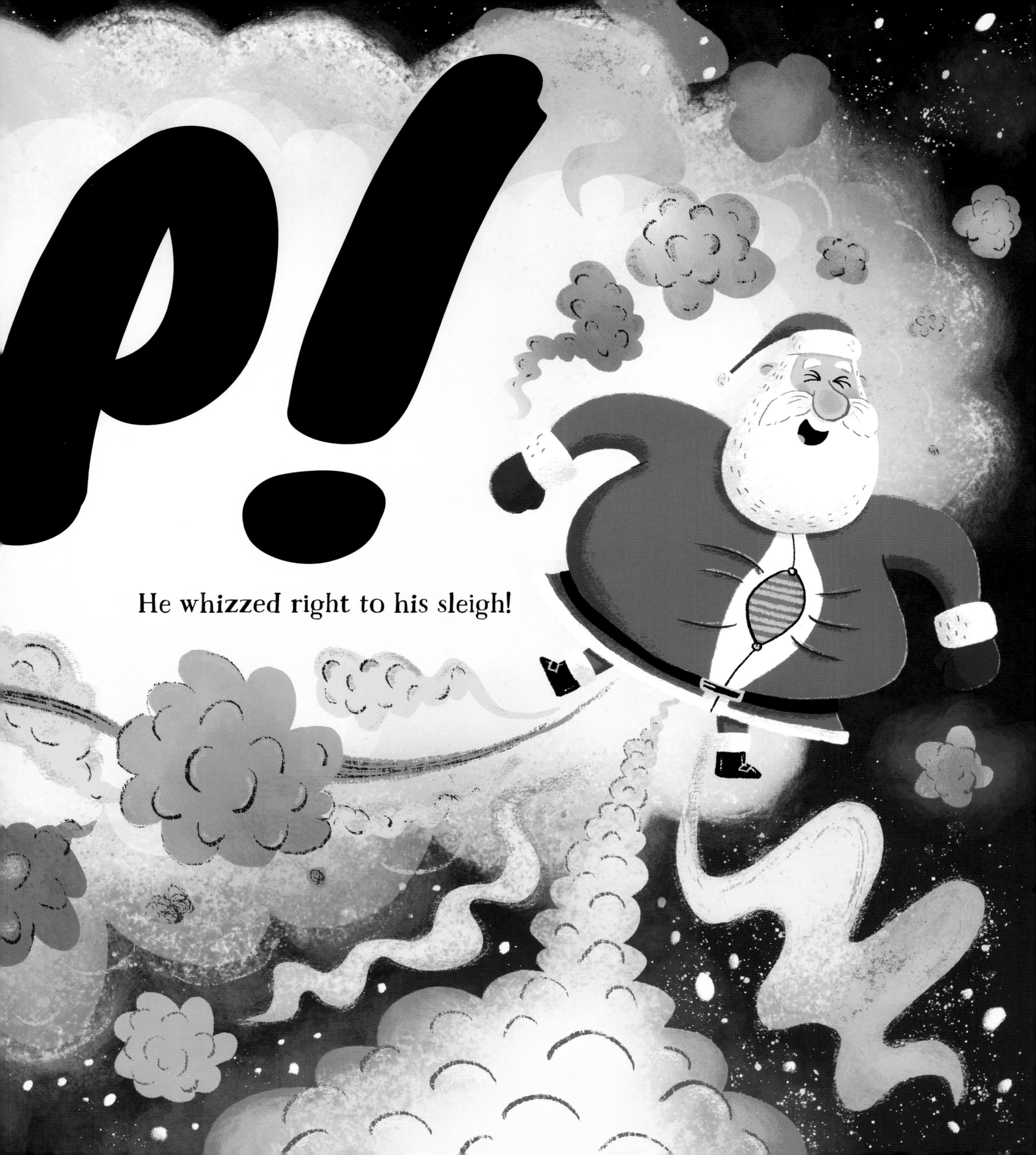
p!

He whizzed right to his sleigh!

"Oh no!" Ellie said, "Those poor people below."
But Santa just winked. "Time to give them a show!"
He started it off and then Ellie joined in . . .

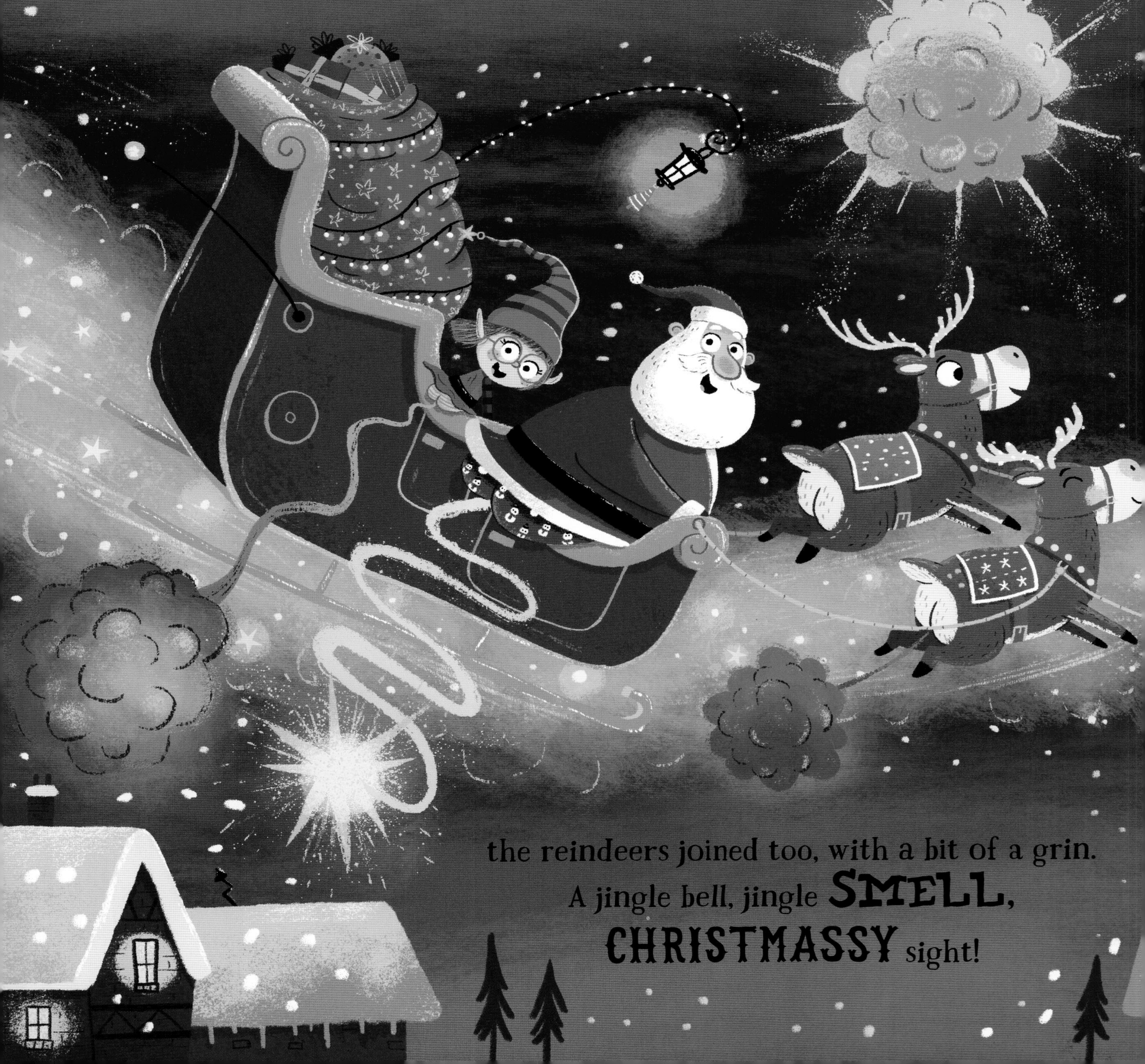

the reindeers joined too, with a bit of a grin.
A jingle bell, jingle **SMELL**,
CHRISTMASSY sight!

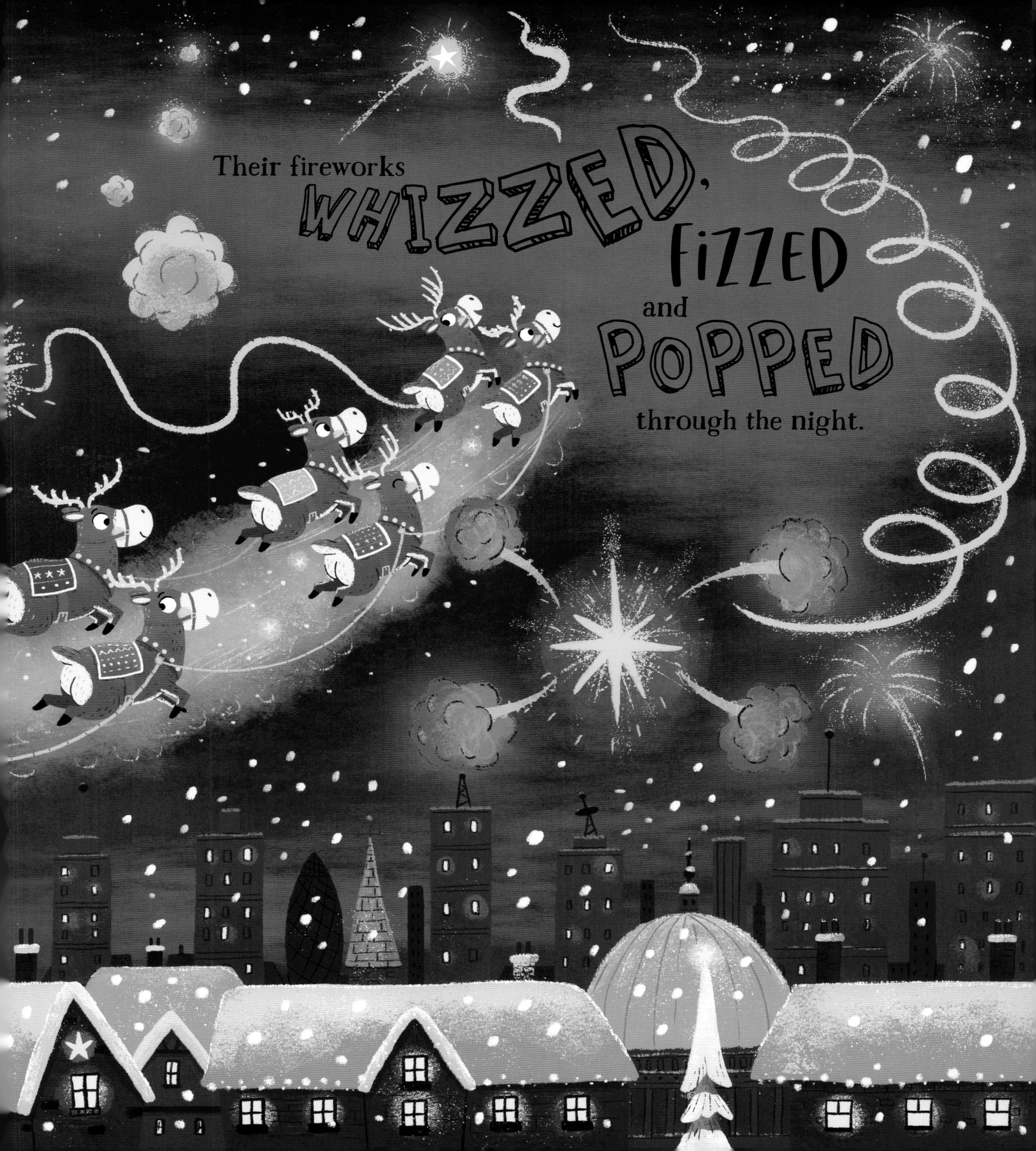

Their fireworks WHIZZED, FIZZED and POPPED through the night.

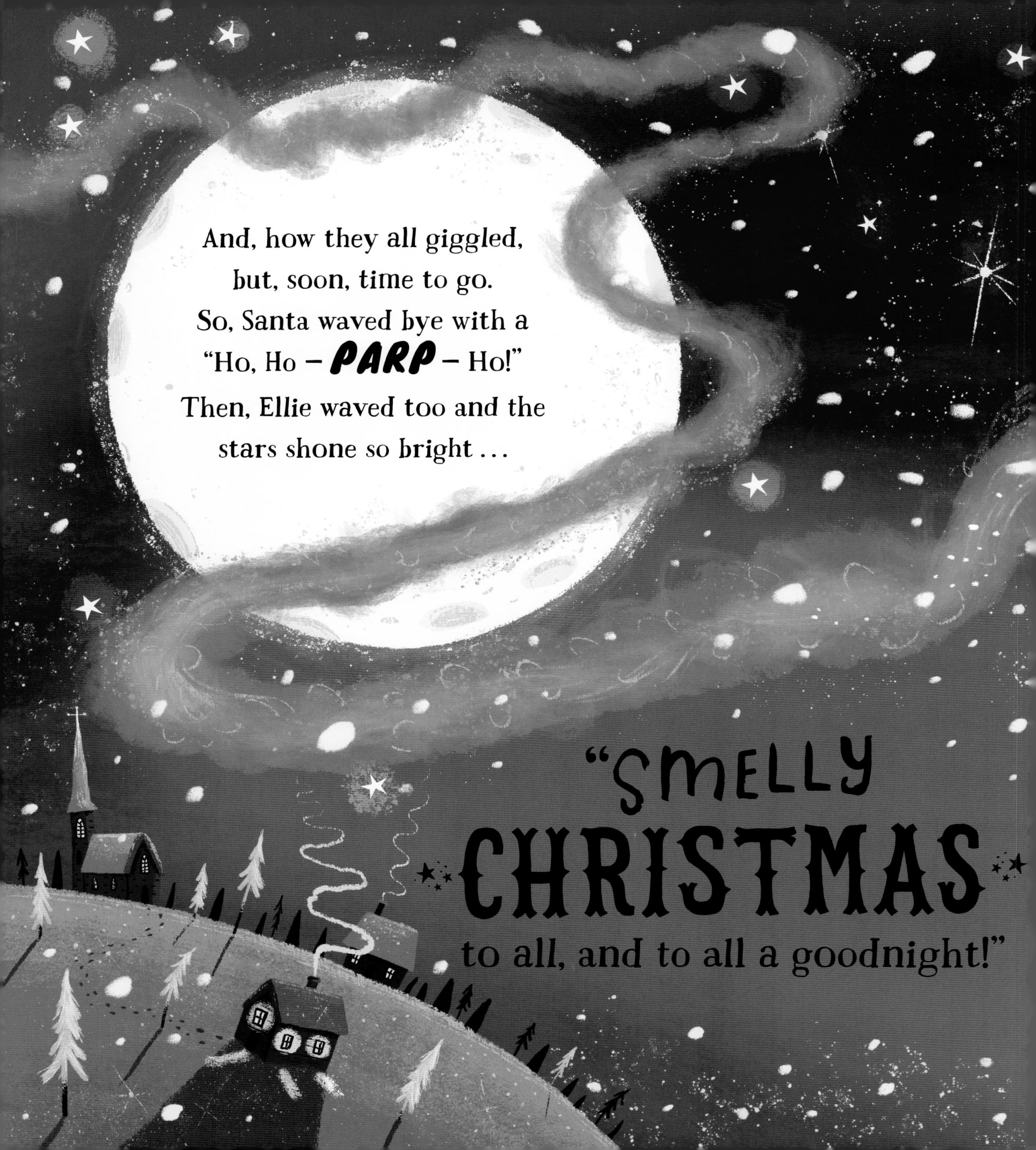

And, how they all giggled,
but, soon, time to go.
So, Santa waved bye with a
"Ho, Ho – **PARP** – Ho!"
Then, Ellie waved too and the
stars shone so bright …

"Smelly
CHRISTMAS
to all, and to all a goodnight!"

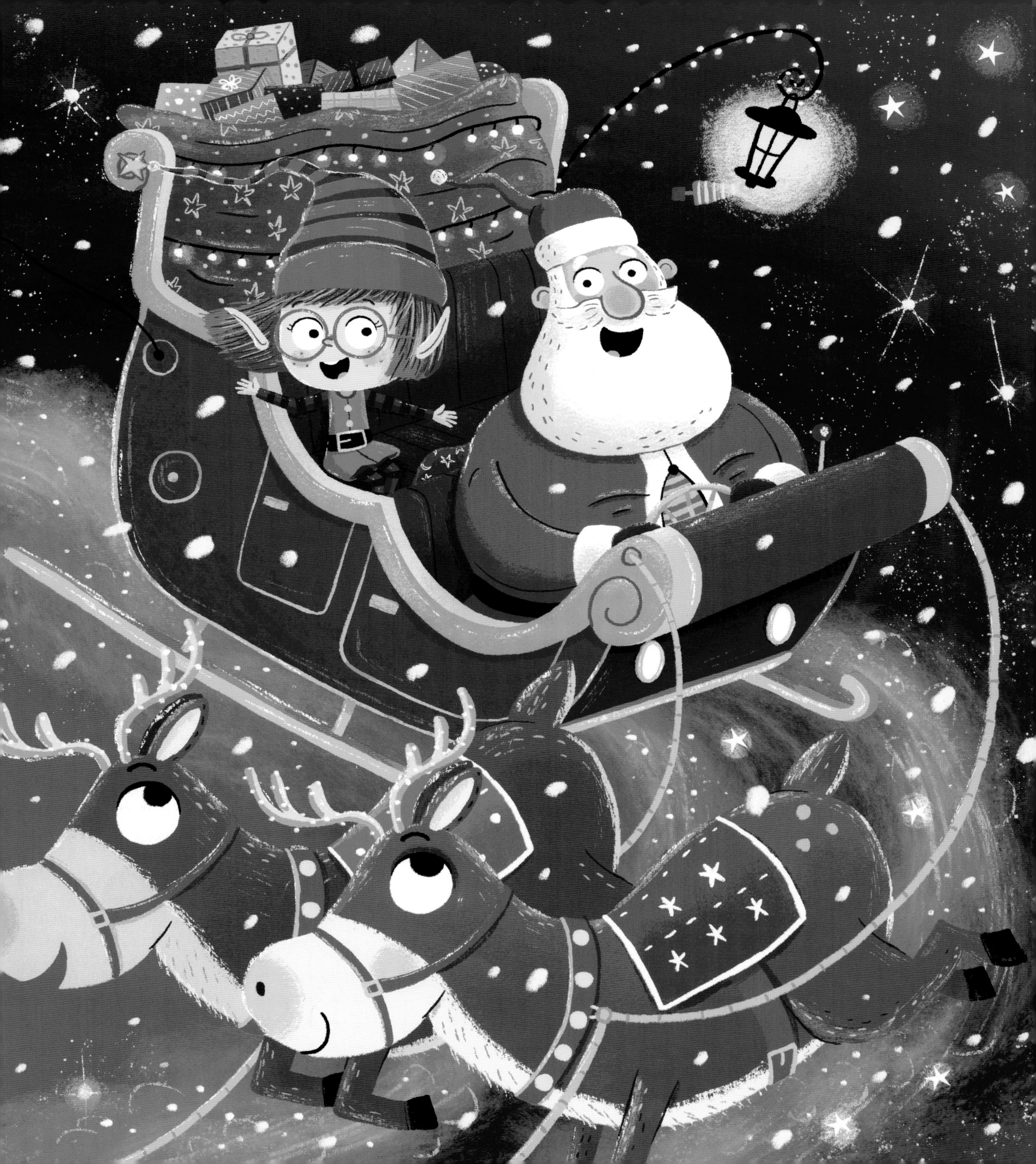

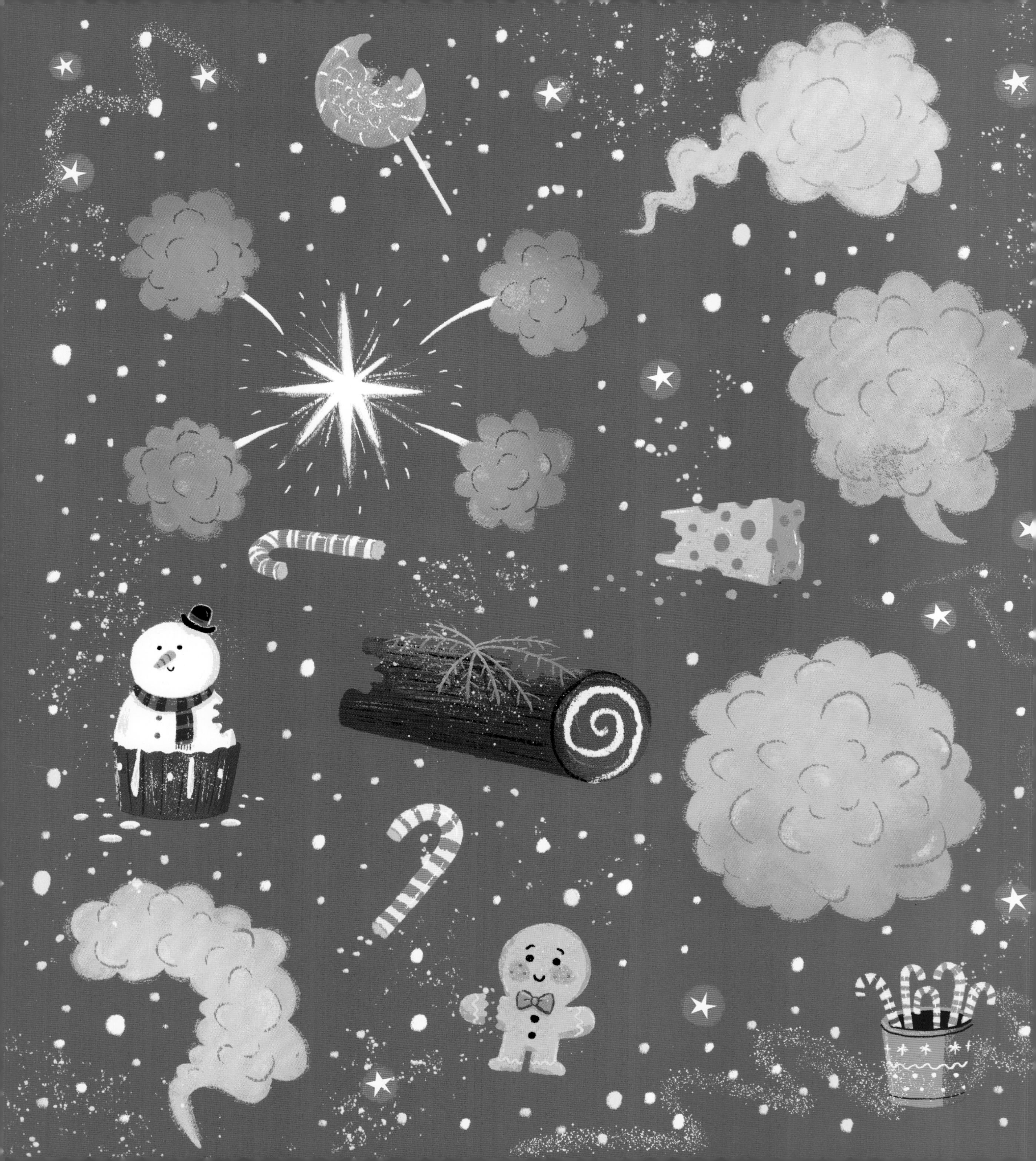

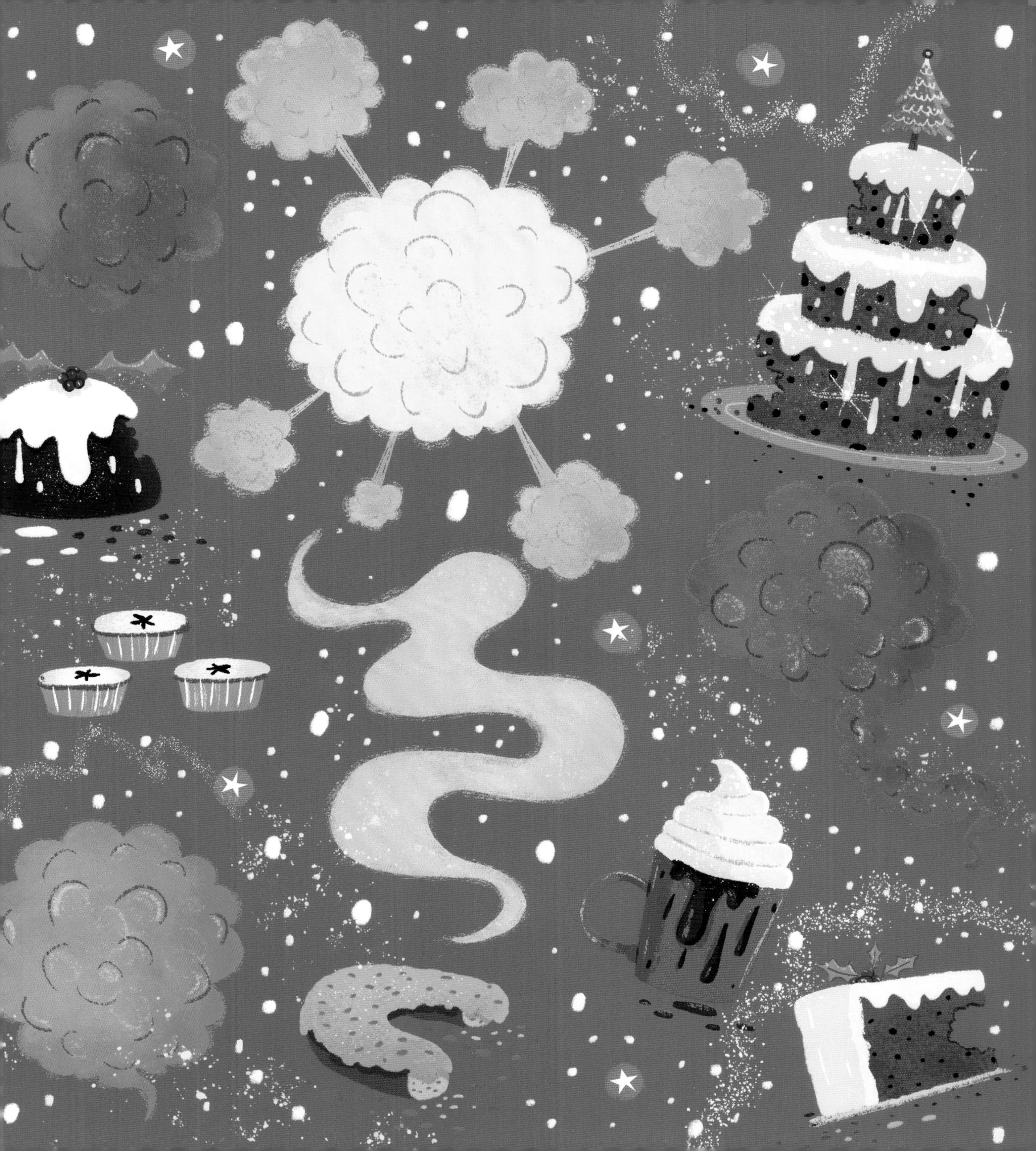